GERTRUDE

"Jed?" she said.

"Yes." I paused. "I don't know you," I said.

"I'm . . . Gertrude. Now you do," she replied.

"Look," I said, "Gertrude"—I glanced at my watch—"this is a little odd and I'm supposed to be at tennis practice."

"Don't you have to take the Camaro home first?"

I stared at her.

"Your father's gonna be worried about it, yes?"

I swallowed.

"He'll be at your big house on Ridgeline waiting for you, right?" she added. "And then you have tennis practice."

My heart started to go *poomp-poomp, poomp-poomp*. I wondered if she was one of those insane I-know-what-you-did-last-summer kind of chicks.

"What do you know about it?" I shot back.

"A lot," Gertrude said. "If your father ain't home, I can guess where he is."

ALSO BY WILL WEAVER

claws

A NOVEL BY
WILL WEAVER

HARPERTEMPEST
An Imprint of HarperCollinsPublishers

Claws

Copyright © 2003 by Will Weaver

Library of Congress Cataloging-in-Publication Data
Weaver, Will.
    Claws : a novel / by Will Weaver.
      p. cm.
    Summary: Jed and Laura, two popular Minnesota high school students,
find their seemingly perfect lives suddenly in chaos when they discover
that each has a parent who is having an affair with the other.
    ISBN 0-06-009473-7 — ISBN 0-06-009474-5 (lib. bdg.)
    ISBN 0-06-009475-3 (pbk.)
    [1. Adultery—Fiction. 2. Family problems—Fiction. 3. High schools—
Fiction. 4. Schools—Fiction. 5. Minnesota—Fiction.] I. Title.
PZ7.W3623 Cl 2003   2002023844
[Fic]—dc21   CIP
                                         AC

Typography by Karin Paprocki
❖
First paperback edition, 2004
Visit us on the World Wide Web!
www.harpertempest.com

"...Life will sooner or later show its claws."
—Anton Chekhov

(from his story "Gooseberries")

CHAPTER ONE

Say life is good. Say you're finally sixteen and things are coming together. In the space of six months you got your driver's license, grew sideburns, landed a major girlfriend, made number-one singles in varsity tennis. Like pieces of a puzzle—a bird, a cloud, blue sky, yellow sun—things are falling into place. Your two sisters are finally gone to college, which means you have the upstairs all to yourself. Not only that, it's May in Minnesota: Spring is here.

Sweet.

But it gets better.

Your father, Gary, has begun to let you drive his 1969 Camaro instead of the old family Honda. Your cruising in the big Chevy with Cassie, your senior girlfriend (you're a junior), drives your enemies wild. Beefy football players, no-neck wrestlers, greasy motor heads—they all want to crush your skull.

Sweet and sweeter.

Driving the Camaro also keeps you and your father close.

In fact, you and he talked about how some fathers buy their teenagers' affections with a car—but *certainly* not him. You both laughed. You have that kind of relationship with him; you've always been tight.

In fact, your friends admire both your parents. They don't mind hanging out at your house because your father (an architect) jokes with them, which means he takes them seriously, and your mother (an attorney) bakes them ginger cookies and chocolate bars. Even Cassie says, "You've got the *coolest* parents."

"Thanks," you say, trying for aw-shucks awkward. But you know she's right. First, you have two parents. Lots of kids you know have parents who are splitso—one lives here, one lives there, you know the scene. But Gary and Andrea have been married forever; they're the most successful couple you can think of.

Your father's a freelance home designer with a focus on lakefront and log houses; when he's not drawing a house, he publishes magazine articles on the subject. His office is at home, which means he was always there after school to greet you with milk and cookies. Pleasantville all the way. Your mother is a partner in the largest law firm in the city, and has more clients than she can handle. She works long hours, and is involved in several civic organizations, and gets kind of stressed out at times, but she makes a lot of money—probably way more than your father—which is not a problem with him.

Me? My name's Jed Berg. I'll get to me soon enough. First I need you to see my parents—like I'm trying to right now. The only thing I know for sure about parents is this: It's a free country except for them. You can change everything about yourself—your looks, your friends, your room, your job—but not your parents. Having parents is like arriving at a restaurant where there's no menu. You eat what's put on the table. There are no substitutions, no returns.

My father, at six foot three, is still taller than me but not by much anymore. He has a runner's physique and an outdoorsy look: flannel shirts, cap, trimmed salt-and-pepper beard, squinty blue eyes. Mother is smaller, darker, fine boned. She's also in great shape, plays tennis at the downtown health club. She has penetrating brown eyes—as dark as rifle bores—and when she turns them on you full force, you're dead. My mother dresses J. Crew, successful businesswoman; my father wears jeans and Polarfleece vests. We live here in Duluth, the Gateway to the North Shore (my father grew up here). My mother grew up in north Minneapolis; she's not close with her family. In fact, I hardly know my grandparents on her side. To be honest, they're kind of crude and trashy, which you'd never guess when

3

you look at my mother.

We have an embarassingly nice house on Ridgeline Boulevard that looks out over Lake Superior. I remember moving in—I was about eight—and the house felt like a castle. That first night all five of us sat out on the upstairs balcony and ate popcorn and watched the lights. Iron-ore freighters winked and blinked on the black surface of the great lake like satellites in the night sky; closer in, at bay front, the lights on the Duluth-Superior Lift Bridge sparkled like a square necklace. It felt like Christmas Eve every night. That first summer we spent a lot of family time there, watching the night lights of the city and bay. It was sweet. Then we all got busy, or older, and the view and the lights weren't as important anymore.

What can I tell you about my sisters, Anne and Melanie? To be honest, I'm glad they're gone. They fought all the time with my mother, who I think was too much on their cases. She just never let up—about eating enough, about picking up their rooms, about getting As in school, about "being some-body," as she put it. I tried to stay out of it, as did my father. This year has been great with both of them off to college. They hardly ever come home. Which is a little sad, I would guess, for my parents.

But hey, enough about them. As I said, my name is Jed. My grade-school friends still call me "Jed-eye," but let's

4

stick with Jed. It goes better with my sideburns.

Today, during our routine leaving-for-school conversation, my father said, "The usual, Jed, all right?" He narrowed his eyes slightly.

"For sure," I answered. "The usual" was code for rules about driving the Chevy. They included no unreasonable acceleration (i.e., drag racing), no excessive cruising (the big block V-8 engine had a tendency to overheat at slow speed), no more than two people in the car, and so on.

"Come home and park it right after school!" he called to me—as usual.

I was already in the garage. I settled into the seat, gripped the huge steering wheel, then fired the engine. It was always a thrill. As the horsepower rumble coursed up my spine, I had my Weird Thought of the Day: Life could never get any better.

After school, tucked under the windshield wiper on the Chevy was a note. A small piece of paper, folded several times.

"Hey—a love letter!" said Bobby Wheeler, my neighborhood pal from down the hill; he was also on the tennis team, though probably just because I was. Bobby grabbed at the note, but I snatched it first. Regular school notebook paper with a torn, fuzzy edge.

"Who's it from?" Bobby asked.

"Jed-eye's got a valentine," called Nate Fenson, a wrestler. "Must be one of them rich tennis girls." Nate and I had been in classes together ever since kindergarten, which now was the only possible thing we had in common. Nate's parents were splitso, his mother ran a day care from home, and he had become a complete troglodyte. Behind Nate, homing in on the Chevy, came a small gang of motor heads in greasy caps. I glanced at the note.

Cassie really wants to see you. Perkins at 3:30.
A Friend

Strange. I was sure Cassie had spring soccer practice.

"Maybe it's from Ms. Smythe," one of Nate's friends said. All the motor heads began to grunt like gorillas. Ms. Smythe was the new ninth-grade English teacher, single and blond.

"'Hot for the teacher!'" Nate crowed. He accompanied himself with a pathetic (as in muscle-bound) air guitar.

"Give her a ride in your daddy's car, Berg," someone said.

"I'd give her another kind of ride," one them added, and there was coarse laughter as they crowded around the Camaro.

"Wish my old man was rich," Kenny Rognstad said. He gripped the side mirror.

"Me, too." One of the wrestlers began to rock the Camaro side to side.

6

"Hey, easy on the sheet metal!" I said.

"What you gonna do about it, tennis boy?"

"Gotta go," I said cheerfully to the troglodytes. "Come on, Bobby." I couldn't leave the poor schmuck; the carnivores would rip him apart. Crunching the note into my pocket, I quickly unlocked the driver's door and then the steering-wheel Club. The cap boys and wrestlers slowly turned away to their pickups, poking chew into their cheeks and ignoring us—until I fired the engine: In the mirror I saw them turn as one to look.

"Eat me, losers!" I muttered. I really hated them sometimes.

"Cool," Bobby said, looking over his shoulder at the jealous truck boys.

I eased the Camaro into first gear, then drove toward the parking-lot exit. A couple of knuckleheads lurched their rust buckets in front of me, knowing I wouldn't challenge them for first out—not in the Camaro. Bobby hung out his window and gave them a double one-finger salute.

"Don't!" I said sharply to Bobby. I grabbed his shirt and yanked him back inside. People acted strangely in the Chevy. Even Cassie sat up stiffly and kept fluffing her blond hair when she rode with me. It was one of the several small things I didn't like about her; however, with a body like hers, character flaws were easy to overlook.

As we rumbled down Division Street (I had to make at least one loop before heading home), Bobby said, "So, really, who was that note from?"

I tossed it his way.

He uncrumpled it. "A 'friend.' Of Cassie's." Then he looked at me. "It's the car, you know."

"What about it?"

"Cassie Swanson, student council prez, Show Choir queen? You think she's going to give you the time of day if you were driving a rusty eighty-two Vega?"

"Hey—she's attracted to my mind, my personality."

"Right," Bobby said with sarcasm. "Say, can you drop me off at work?"

I drove on a half block. "I guess," I finally said. I don't know why I was so nice to him.

I dropped Bobby off at Rug Remnant City, where he worked after school; he waved and then stood there, watching me drive off. A stubby bowlegged kid with a bad haircut, who should have been a wrestler. Pathetic. Bobby was such a loser, he didn't even understand he was a loser. Maybe that's why I was still loyal to him. That and the fact we'd built a lot of snowmen and forts together back in the day. In my rearview mirror, I saw Bobby's shoulders slump as he turned to head inside Remnant City. He was actually not that bad at tennis—the kind of dogged player who made up in hustle for what he lacked in finesse. If he hadn't had to work so much (his second job was delivering Domino's pizzas) and miss practice, he might even have made number-two singles.

It was already 3:18 P.M., which made it tight getting home on time, parking the Chevy, then walking the six blocks to Perkins, so I drove directly to the restaurant. I parked at the far edge of the lot under the giant American flag. It was tattered at the edges and rattled in the breeze; the wind blew a lot up near Ridgeline. Students straggled in, but no Cassie. I checked my watch, went inside.

"Just one?" the hostess said. She was middle-aged and had tired eyes.

"I guess. For now," I added. But she had already turned away, and so I followed her.

I took my booth and waited.

And waited.

After five minutes of sitting by myself and looking like a loser, I suddenly understood I'd been had. Somebody's idea of joke. I let out an annoyed sound and started to leave—I had to get to tennis practice by 3:45—when a girl plopped into my booth. Not any girl. A punk chick with pink hair.

I froze. "Hello?" I said.

She stared at me. Bright-pink hair above heavy black eye shadow plus enough metal in her nose to make airport detectors beep at fifty yards. Dark, gothy clothes. But

9

weirdly tanned—and strong—wrists and forearms.

"Jed?" she said.

"Yes."

"Cassie couldn't come."

I narrowed my eyes. "Are you two friends or something?"

"Or something," she said.

I paused. "I don't know you," I said.

"I'm . . . Gertrude. Now you do," she replied.

There was more silence.

"Look," I said, "Gertrude"—I glanced at my watch—"this is a little odd and I'm supposed to be somewhere."

"Don't you have to take the Camaro home first?"

I stared at her.

"Your father's gonna be worried about it, yes?"

I swallowed.

"He'll be at your big house on Ridgeline waiting for you, right?" she added. "And then you have tennis practice."

My heart started to go *poomp-poomp, poomp-poomp*. I wondered if she was one of those insane I-know-what-you-did-last-summer kind of chicks. Not that I did anything last summer except play tennis.

"What do you know about it?" I shot back.

"A lot," Gertrude said. "If your father ain't home, I can guess where he is."

I paused. "Who the hell are you?"

She paused. "I could be a brain fart. Or bad cafeteria food. Or a gas bubble. But sorry to say I'm real."

"That's it—I'm gone." One lurch and I was halfway to the door. Behind, I heard her metal bracelets jingling as she scrambled to follow me. She didn't catch up until I was near the Chevy; there she lunged ahead of me and blocked the driver's door.

"Listen—you and I have something in common," she said. She turned and braced both hands on the car.

"I can't think of what it would be—and please step away from the car." My heartbeat was at high rpm.

"No. Wait, I'm not trying to weird you out." For a half second her voice sounded different—almost normal—not at all like a creepy goth chick's.

I paused. "So what the hell are you trying to do?"

"I'm trying to tell you something," she said.

"Like what?"

There was another pause. Dead air. Then she blurted, "Your father is sleeping with my mother."

CHAPTER TWO

At home, my dad was in his office. Like I knew he would be. Sitting in his regular chair below the framed gray wolf drawing and with blueprints spread out across his desk. Like always. He looked up from his computer screen with a glazed, squinty, I'm-deep-in-a-project look. Like always.

"Hey, Dad."

"Jeddy." He glanced back to his computer—there was text on the screen—and with a keystroke cleared it. "So," he said, turning fully to me. "How was school?"

"Samo," I said.

"Good," he said.

I waited.

"What!?" he added, smiling a little.

"Thanks for letting me drive the Chevy."

He looked quickly toward the driveway. "Everything okay?"

"Sure, no problem."

"Whew! Good. You scared me there for a second."

I nodded toward the screen. "Whatcha working on?"

"Just some client e-mail. Nothing serious."

I nodded.

"Any homework?" he asked.

"Algebra. English. History. The usual."

"Okay, good." He seemed more distracted than usual, though maybe it was just me. "Say, don't you have tennis practice?" he added.

"No," I said. "They're . . . resurfacing the court."

"Okay," he said. There was a pause. "But your Monday went all right," he said; his eyes glanced back to his screen.

I thought of the goth chick. "Yeah, no problem."

That night I couldn't stop thinking about Weird Girl. I needed to slow down my brain, so after the house was quiet and my parents asleep, I went on-line. I scanned through a couple of adult sites—hey, it's hard to avoid them—and looked at naked people. I have a computer in my bedroom, which all guidelines for teens and computers say is a no-no: *Keep the computer in a central location in the house; that way, the teenager is less likely to access questionable material from the Internet.* Blah blah blah. My parents and I had our porn talk years ago. Mother said it was not possible (she knows her way around computers) to prevent me from looking at porn; therefore, I had to find "my own relationship" with it—ideally none or very little—considering how it demeaned women.

My father's contribution was to tell a story. He told about his father (my grandpa Walter) who, upon catching Gary (then a kid) with a naughty magazine, went out and bought a whole bag of raunchy mags and told him to read them until he got sick of them. My father finished the story with a laugh. My mother was not amused. My father shrugged and said, "Hey, it wasn't the worst parenting idea in the world."

Which I found out to be true.

When I first got my own computer in my room—I was thirteen—I looked at porn until my eyeballs went dry. The rudest, nastiest sites, day and night I was there. But after about two weeks, I got tired of it. I mean, how many nude pictures of inflated-air-bag blondes and naked beefy guys can you look at? Still, before I got really bored with porn, my grades started to slip plus I tended to slink around feeling lousy about myself. Kind of like I was having a bad hair day but on the inside. Soon enough I could see I had to figure out some kind of (my mother was right) "personal guidelines" in terms of porn. So I came up with Jed Berg's Teen Porn Code:

1. No hard-core XXX-rated stuff. That shit will seriously rot your brain. Those people are sad—the site owners and Web masters more than the models—and eventually their sadness gets inside you.

2. No "voyeur-dorm, coed-house" fixed-cam sites. A sure

way to weird yourself out with real girls is to sit around for hours and watch what they do in private, like brush their teeth and clip their toenails and take dumps and change their tampons. It tends to take the magic out of dating.

3. A little nudity, sure. Who doesn't like looking at Australian girls naked on the beach (summer there) during the long winter in Duluth, Minnesota?

3. But fifteen minutes of this per day, maximum. All inclusive, no exceptions, no excuses.

4. Overtime minutes (hey, I'm only human) must be deducted from the next day's fifteen minutes. Accordingly, unused minutes can be banked for later use. For example, a five-day family vacation at the lake cabin means, back at home, seventy-five minutes of guilt-free Girls-Gone-Wild-on-Spring-Break.

5. To keep from going over personal time limits, safeguards must be in place.

Me, I had a routine. I cued up my stereo, which was on the opposite side of my room, to come on in fifteen minutes with the worst music imaginable. Right now, it was set to an old 'N Sync CD that belonged to one of my sisters (even she left it behind when she went off to college). When 'N Sync came on, believe me, I always dove across the room to hit eject—which broke any potential porn enslavement.

This all might seem a bit OCD, but hey—whatever works, right?

Anyway, tonight I was on-line looking for new Alyssa Milano photos (lots of fake ones out there), when the you've-got-mail icon flashed.

It was after midnight. Probably Bobby, who was a night owl and a major gamer: Nintendo, SimCity, you name it. A total addict. His latest thing was Sims, which was all about creating a family and buying them things. Sometimes he'd send me a snapshot of his "family" and go on about them like they were real people. Spare me. Enough already, I always told him. In my humble opinion, looking at a little soft-core porn on occasion was way better than being a gamer. I went to my e-mail.

Just to show you I'm not crazy, see attachment.
Gertrude

I stared at the name.

At the note.

My brain started to rattle.

In school, my English teacher, Mr. Stinson, always talked about literary characters and their "life-defining moments"; this felt like one of them—like my life was about to change.

Trouble was, my life didn't need changing: My life was perfect the way it was.

I swallowed, then clicked on the attachment; it was impossible not to.

A photo began to download. My stomach started to churn, my heartbeat to rattle in my ears. The photo grew the head, then shoulders, of my father—and another woman. He was dressed in his usual flannel shirt. The woman was blond, and part of her face was electronically lollipopped to protect her identity. She and my father were standing facing each other, talking; behind them was blue water, a lake. My father and the woman were smiling at each other; they looked really happy about something. However, they weren't doing anything. They were just looking at each other. Talking, for God's sakes. I let out a long breath. I kept scanning the photo for incriminating stuff but found nothing. There wasn't much background, either; the photo had been closely cropped, as if Weird Gertrude wanted to show as little as possible of the setting.

I focused on the blond woman. Unless she was standing on something, she was tall—over five foot ten, I'd say, and big. A large woman. Kind of thick with big shoulders. She did not appear that pretty—certainly not as pretty as my mom. I looked at the photo for a long time, but there was nothing more to be seen.

I squinted at the e-mail URL. A Hotmail address. No telling where it was from.

I hit Reply and typed,

Two people talking. So?

I sat and drummed my fingers. I got my reply within a minute.

I've got other photos where they're doing more than talking.
Gertrude

I cleared the screen, emptied the cache, powered down, got in bed all in one sequence. I lay there in the dark. Motionless. Thinking.

Then, I suppose to prove something to myself, I got up, tiptoed down the hall to my parents' room. Their doorway, half open as usual, glowed with faint light. That was from the tiny seahorse night-light (my mother's side) brought back from one of their vacations. In its dim, pinkish-orange light I saw my parents' bed. Both of them were lying there, as usual. My mother was curled toward one wall, my father to the other. He snored softly. As usual. I stared at them for a long moment, then began to turn away—but not before my mother sat up suddenly. "Jeddy! " she exclaimed. "What's wrong?"

Back in my room 'N Sync came on full volume.

CHAPTER THREE

What's wrong? I thought fast. "I——had a nightmare. I guess. I don't know . . ." I mumbled as if half asleep. Talk about an embarrassing moment——a sixteen-year-old peeping on his parents.

"Do you want to get into bed with Mommy and Daddy?" she mumbled; her eyelids were drooping even as she spoke.

"What!?" I laughed. My mother blinked and woke up for real.

"Huh? What did I say?" she asked.

My dad was half awake now. "Whazz going on?"

"Nothing, go back to sleep."

"Trouble with the Chevy?" Dad said, suddenly wide-awake. He swung his legs out of bed.

"No, I haven't driven anywhere. Please, it's nothing."

"Jeddy had a nightmare," my mother explained; she was more awake now. "Then I said something——what did I say?" she asked.

"You don't want to know," I said. "Really—go back to sleep."

"You sure you're okay?" she asked.

"I'm sure. Good night."

In the morning I hoped no one remembered last night, but two sips into her coffee, my mother suddenly turned to me. "You had a nightmare last night."

I shrugged. "Or something. It was weird."

"You came into our room just like you were small." She smiled. "When you were five, you'd always just stand there in the dark, sniffling, until I'd wake up."

"Thanks a lot," I said wryly. I reached for the toast. "I must have been sleepwalking."

"You woke up too," my mother said to my father.

"Me? I don't remember that," he said, snagging the sports section just ahead of me.

"Nothing new there," my mother replied.

We went on with breakfast. The morning sun shone into the nook, as it always will in a house designed by Garrett Berg; everything was in its place, as it had to be in Andrea Berg's tidy house; and the Cheerios tasted as nutty and crunchy as they always did. I wondered if the punk chick and her e-mail possibly were a bad dream.

"So what's up at school today?" my mother asked, giving

the clock a sideways glance. She leaned toward the refriger-ator and its small mirror to check her hair. Her dark leather briefcase sat poised by the door.

"The usual."

"The *usual*," she said.

"*Samo*," my father said. They were both good at imitating me, which was annoying.

"Well," I began, "we're reading Hawthorne in English, focusing on his use of allegory; we're investigating the Napoleonic period in history, focusing on Napoleon's major error in expanding his eastern front into Russia during the winter, a mistake the Germans, of course, were to repeat during World War II; and we're doing proofs in advanced algebra; static electricity experiments in physics; and nothing at all in civics."

"Okay, okay!" she said.

"She's just checking to see if you actually attend school," my father observed, rattling the sports section.

"Hey, I'm sure you'd know if I wasn't."

"Maybe, maybe not," my mother said as she double-checked the contents of her briefcase. "I meet families in my job where nobody has a clue about what the others are doing."

My father's eyes flickered up from his paper to my mother, then back down. "The Cubs won in fourteen innings," he said. There was a moment of weirdness in the house, as if something dark had flitted past—like the shadow of an air-plane when you're outside on a sunny day—this ragged shadow racing at incredible speed.

"Fourteen innings," I said.

"Well, I'm off, gang," Mother said cheerfully, coming around to give us both a kiss. As she leaned her face down to my father's, I looked away.

At school I found Bobby. I told him about the punk chick with pink hair (leaving out, of course, the weird stuff). "You know any girl like that?"

He thought. Then pretended to pick his nose as if it helped him think. "Not really. There's a few gothy types in ninth grade, but none that strange. Maybe she goes to Oakleaf."

I considered that. Oakleaf was an alternative school for losers who had gotten in trouble—car theft, drugs, what-ever—and now couldn't attend regular high school.

"But then how would she know Cassie?"

"Ask Cassie," Bobby replied, and slid off to chat up some girls who were way out of his league.

I thought about that as I watched Bobby get shot down. He was not dumb, but there was a nervous, scared part inside him. He was probably going to end up selling carpets all his life, but hey, that was his problem.

I didn't see Cassie until lunch, where she disengaged

herself from the senior crowd and came my way. "Hi, Jed."

"Hi, kid," I said. This was our inside joke about her being older than me. She had perfect teeth, perfect skin (I'd never seen a pimple), and some perfume that always made my knees weak. However, when she got really close, something always felt missing—some small thing I couldn't name—and this helped me carry on normal conversations with her.

"Did you drive today?" she asked.

"Sorry, walked."

She stuck out her lower lip in mock pout. "Too bad. I've got a tanning appointment downtown after school, and then I have to get back to soccer. Oh well, *somebody* will give me a ride."

We chitchatted; then, pretending it just popped into my head, I asked, "Hey, do you know a girl with pink hair? Real punky? Lots of face metal?"

She drew back slightly. "No. Nobody like that, for sure." The corners of her perfect mouth turned down a notch. Cassie hung out only with preppy types. Like me, I guess.

"Okay," I said easily.

"Why?"

"Oh it's nothing. I just ran into this weird chick who mentioned your name."

"Strange," Cassie said.

"Probably the drugs," I replied. "Her, not me."

She laughed. "She's probably from Oakleaf."

I think my sense of humor was part of what Cassie liked about me. She was smart in a mathematical kind of way, but irony impaired, which is no small matter.

"Hey, I've got to go," I said, checking my watch, pretending I was late for something. "See you later?" My whoa-look-at-the-time! technique was another personal achievement that I share here: If you want to be successful with girls, particularly with the busiest girls, the ones involved in everything (who also happen to be prettiest, yes?), you have to act busy yourself. In fact, you have to act busier than them. Act like there's really no time to talk—at least right now. Girls love guys who don't have time for them.

"Sure, Jed." She touched my arm. "Call me on my cell. Soon."

"Okay." My knees went rubbery but managed to get me swiveled around and headed in the other direction to my own "appointment."

Which was cafeteria pizza. At the nearest table were Bobby and some short junior girls. My class. So to speak.

"'Call me—soon!'" Bobby crooned.

"Oh, I will!" sighed Chrissy, a girl from my grade. The junior girls I hung around with all hated "Miss Cassie," as they called her; however, they all dressed and acted like

24

her every chance they got.

"Shut up," I hissed at them, but I couldn't keep a goofy smile off my face.

The rest of the day went all right mainly because I managed to put pink-haired Gertrude out of my head. English class was the last period. We finished the Hawthorne story "Young Goodman Brown," which "as you know" (Mr. Stinson's pet phrase to make us feel less stupid) is about this Puritan guy, Goodman Brown, who takes a late-night walk on the wild side. Now we were supposed to figure out *meaning*.

"Sure it's about the goodman's walk into the forest—perhaps actual, perhaps an imaginary forest—but in the end what is the story *really* about?" Mr. Stinson pressed. He was a graying, ponytailed English teacher who wore jeans and leather vests and cowboy boots to prove that you can like poetry and still be a real man.

There was silence in the room.

He sighed. "Okay people. If you'll recall, late at night, deep in the forest, Goodman Brown encounters most of the revered, pious people of his village. Even his own wife, Faith, is out there in the woods," Mr. Stinson added. "There are weird noises, a bonfire, a cane that wriggles like a snake—what are we to make of all this?"

"'Shrooms," somebody muttered. There was laughter.

Mr. Stinson was unfazed. "Hawthorne's writing style is

sort of druggy in spots, but I'm less interested in style than in larger *meaning*," he said. "That's what we're after today."

More silence.

"Okay, then. Let's read the last page aloud." He looked up. "Anyone?"

After long silence, I raised my chin in the faintest of nods. It was a character flaw of mine, helping out a teacher stuck in dead air. But I had my reasons. At least half of the people in my class must have missed *Sesame Street*, *Reading Rainbow*, and possibly elementary school altogether. When the losers read aloud, it was too painful. I couldn't listen.

"Thanks, Jed!" Mr. Stinson said.

"Suck-up," Bobby whispered.

"Start after he wakes up in the forest the next morning," Mr. Stinson requested.

I began: "'The next morning, young Goodman Brown came slowly into the streets of Salem village staring around him like a bewildered man. . . .'"

I read on, through the part where Goodman Brown sees the good and pious people, though now he doesn't trust them. In church he no longer hears the hymns but only an "anthem of sin." In his mind, everyone is corrupt, fake, and evil. I suddenly stopped reading in mid sentence.

There was silence. I sensed faces looking up, turning toward me.

Mr. Stinson said, "Jed?"

I stared at him. All I could think about was my father and the big blond woman—the way they were staring at each other in the photo.

"Did you lose your place?" Stinson asked.

"No."

"Picking up a rogue cable channel?" Bobby asked.

"Enough, Bobby," Mr. Stinson said sharply.

"Sorry," I said; I gathered my wits and read quickly through to the ending. It was the part where, many years later, Goodman Brown's family carried him, "a hoary corpse," to his grave. I finished:

"'They carved no hopeful verse upon his tombstone; for his dying hour was gloom.'"

There was silence in the room.

"What a downer," somebody said.

"I agree," said Katie Sorenson. She began to wave her hand. "Mr. Stinson? Why does, like, all the literature we read have, like, really sucky endings?"

"Yeah, why—that's right—why?" several voices chimed.

Praise literary rebellion; it took the focus off me. And Mr. Stinson, a master of *carpe diem*, perked up immediately. "Okay, people, let's talk about tragedy, Aristotelian style," he said. "We went over tragedy in the drama section just last week, remember?"

There was silence.

Actually, I did remember, but I wasn't about to volunteer again for anything.

"Okay. Let's come at Aristotelian tragedy from another direction," Mr. Stinson said. "Consider *Psycho*, *Halloween*, *Scream*, plus all the other horror films, old and new—why are they so popular? Why do we go to them? Why do we love them?"

There was silence.

"Because most people can't deal with the real horror of life, which is boredom," Derek Jones said softly.

Everybody turned. Derek was a pale, long-haired, black-T-shirt guy who mainly played electric guitar in his parents' basement and did serious computer hacking; he seldom spoke. This may have been his first time all year. He was the kind of dude who usually ended up in Oakleaf Alternative School.

Mr. Stinson rapidly stroked his goatee. "Very interesting, Derek. Very French, in a way. You're speaking of what the Existentialist writers would call *ennui*. "

"Or it might be that people are intrinsically violent," Derek continued, not hearing Mr. Stinson, "and since we can't legally kill or stab or blow up anyone, we need violent movies to keep us from going insane."

I flashed forward to Derek's senior-year personal-goals

statement: "I, Derek Jones, hope to be a rock star, or else CEO of my own Internet music production company; or, those failing, a serial killer."

"Movies as vicarious, sublimated violence. Very interesting," Mr. Stinson mused.

"I don't know *what* you're talking about," Katie interjected. "I think people go to horror movies and read Stephen King novels because sometimes we just like to be scared shitless."

Mr. Stinson stared at her.

"What?" Katie said.

"Yes, Katie, exactly!" Mr. Stinson said. He spun into his combination end-zone dance and duck walk, which carried him across the front of the classroom; it was a move he busted whenever there was some kind of intellectual "breakthrough" in class, and he was shameless about it. "Catharsis, Katie—that's what Aristotle called it," Stinson said. "For good mental health, Aristotle believed that we regularly need to purge our emotions."

"I know this chick who purges like twice a day," a girl said from the rear. There was huge laughter.

"Huh? What was that?" Mr. Stinson asked. He paused. His moment was gone, but he was happy; the class had managed to act like it hadn't learned anything, so it was happy; plus everyone had forgotten my momentary possession by the dark forces of Hawthorneian allegory—in short, it was all good. What's more, the bell rang.

"Jed," Mr. Stinson called as class dispersed, "can I see you a sec?"

I sighed and hung back.

"Jed," he said, "when you were reading, you seemed to have some kind of . . . epiphany?"

He was not the most uncool teacher I'd ever had; I had to respect a man who didn't mind making a fool of himself every day in front of large numbers of teenagers.

"Just got to thinking," I said.

"About what?"

"The idea of . . . secret lives." I hadn't meant to go that far; it just slipped out.

He nodded. "We read about them all the time, don't we? Upstanding church secretary embezzles the offering money to pay for her gambling habit. Traveling salesman has a wife and kids in Minneapolis and a wife and kids in Fargo."

I flinched, but in his enthusiasm for Hawthorne, Stinson missed it. "Hawthorne's the man," he said. "He's a bit heavy on Puritan guilt, but he's usually right on the money when it comes to the human heart, and the things people are capable of doing."

"Gotta go," I mumbled.

* * *

30

At home my father was in his office speaking on the phone with someone; "I'll talk to you in a sec," he mouthed to me.

I nodded and slid up to my room. I powered up, went on-line, checked my mail. My heartbeat *poomp-poomp*ed as the messages loaded. Gertrude was back.

I didn't even look at the others; I went straight to her mail.

Don't say I didn't warn you.
Gertrude

Again, I couldn't not open the JPEG. This time——same setting, same blue lake behind——my father was kissing the large blond woman.

CHAPTER FOUR

Once when I was small, about five years old, my father shaved off his beard. He had always worn a beard. When I saw him that day without one, I cried and ran away and hid. I thought he was a fake. Not my real father. Everybody, especially my sisters, got a huge laugh out of this (my father grew back his whiskers as quickly as he could and never fully shaved again). Me, I didn't think it was funny then and still don't.

Now, at family dinner, he felt like that again. A fake father. An impostor. A stranger sitting at our table. I sneaked a closer look at the squint lines around his eyes; at the single horizontal wrinkle across his forehead; at the small scar, pale and curving like a sliver of moon, high on his left cheek. The scar was from my red-and-white Daredevil spoon and its treble hook; it happened during the summer I was six, when he was teaching me how to fish. Sure, all the details matched my real father. But any clever alien or cyborg could replicate lines, wrinkles, and scars. Just as any clever computer geek could cut and paste my father with the blonde.

I took a gulp of milk and tried to get a grip.

"So how was your day?" my mother said to both of us.

My father glanced at me. I pretended to have my mouth full. "Well," my father began, "fairly routine stuff in the building trades. However, this one contractor is driving me crazy."

"Which project?" my mother asked automatically. She passed me the green beans.

"That lake home near Ely. The builder, an older guy, doesn't want to put in the skylights. He says all skylights eventually leak." My father sighed. "I'll probably have to go up there on Friday."

"No, really?" my mother said with disappointment; she finally looked at him.

My father held up his hands in a gesture of helplessness.

"Will you be back Friday night?" she asked.

"I can't say for sure. It's a long drive, and we're behind schedule up there. I'll see how it goes," he said.

"Well, I suppose I've got work I can do Friday night," my mother said.

"If I have to stay over, I'll be back Saturday before noon," my father added. "What about you, Jeddy?" he said. "Anything happen today?"

Well, let's see. Oh yeah—I received this photo of you kissing a giant blond woman.

33

I managed to mumble through a summary of my Wednesday at school.

"And tennis? How did practice go?" my mother interrupted.

"Okay."

"Any interesting challenges?"

"Soren Smith moved up to number-two singles."

"That's that left-handed sophomore?" she said.

I nodded.

"Better be careful," my mother said.

"No threat," I said. I turned back to my food.

"That's the spirit," my mother replied. She took her tennis—and mine—seriously. Until eighth grade I hated playing with her; she was the kind of mother who did not let her kids win. Now that I could beat her, I didn't like that feeling either.

Dinner continued. My mother spoke about her day, a court case involving a warehouse and who or what—the builder or a windstorm—was responsible for cracks in the walls.

"Who owns the building now?" Gary asked.

"It's an auto-body shop," she said. "A family business."

"What are they asking for?"

"For the construction company to fix the walls."

"And if they lose?"

My mother shrugged. "They'll probably have to find

another shop somewhere."

"Tough," my father murmured.

"Life goes on," my mother said, passing me the bread.

"It usually goes on easier for big companies than it does for small business owners," my father countered.

In the silence except for the clink of silverware, I suddenly realized that my father was a Democrat and my mother a Republican. It was amazing that I never thought of that before.

"You're home tonight?" my mother said, turning the focus to me.

"I guess," I said.

"Lots of homework?" my father asked.

"History, algebra, the usual."

He nodded and bent to his food. I watched them eat. Most of our dinner conversations could be put on tape and played back, and no one could tell when they occurred. They'd be like that Bill Murray movie *Groundhog Day*, when events keep repeating themselves. Bobby rented the movie once, had to go to work and didn't finish it, and somehow it got rewound, and then he could never be sure of the spot where he had left off.

"Gotta go," I said, getting up from the table, quickly clearing my plate.

"Homework calling?" my mother said. She gave me her

brown-eyed, penetrating stare.

"Or maybe Cassie?" my father remarked.

I pretended to laugh, then disappeared to my room.

I hid out there, listening to music, trying to concentrate on my homework, until my mother tapped on my door and looked in. "Your father and I have to go a Chamber of Commerce thing. We won't be long. Don't leave algebra for last. There's ice cream bars in the fridge."

"Thanks, Mom." She was wearing a soft-looking brown dress and a bright, flower-patterned scarf draping her left shoulder. In the window light, tiny wrinkles stood out around her eyes. She was pretty. But she also was getting old. She was already forty-five. Or was it forty-six? Her birthday was early in February, but I realized I could not instantly say in what year she was born. My father's birth year either. Each parent, when it was time, had always bought me a birthday card to give to the other. I kept staring at her.

"You look nice tonight," I blurted out.

"Why, Jeddy, thank you!" She came over and gave me a brief hug.

I stared at her.

"Is everything all right?" she asked, narrowing her eyes.

"Sure," I said. "Have a great time."

"We'll try," she said, hoisting an eyebrow briefly, then

smiling a bit. It was code for we-all-know-your-father-doesn't-like-downtown-businesspeople. Then she left.

I lay there. I thought of other things about which my parents disagreed: the Duluth bay foghorn; the Swedish disco group ABBA; art with loons or wolves in it; dressing up for church.

As I lay there, the garage door whirred. I went to my window and looked down to the driveway; my mother's dark Lexus backed out and purred away. Her window was up, my father's down. Add air-conditioning to the list (he said it gave him headaches, and after all, that's why we lived in Duluth, which was naturally air-conditioned).

I lay there. The list of their differences stayed in my head. I wondered about its size in relation to other parents'. Big? Small? I suppose there were other things they disagreed about that I was not aware of, which would make the list still longer. On the other hand, did size count? Wouldn't it be possible for parents to have a huge list of disagreements— but all minor ones? Conversely, couldn't parents have only one area of disagreement—but as wide as the Grand Canyon? My mind was spinning, banging around inside my head. I got up and went downstairs.

I walked through the pale, immaculate living room. I picked up things—the carved Inuit walrus the size of my fist, the Lake Superior agate paperweight—and I put them down.

I went to the wall photograph of my parents. A beach picture. "Cancun," it read. I would have been four, my sisters eight and ten. I tried to remember my parents being away then but couldn't. I remembered the conch shell they brought me, its pink curves, how I could really hear the ocean inside. There they stood, on the beach in Mexico, in faded turquoise water, the surf pounding silently behind them. My father, without sunglasses (add to list) was laughing and had his arm around my mother. My mother wore big, dark sunnies and was standing straighter and smiling only a little—an uncertain smile. Her head was turned a few degrees, as if she were starting to look behind her for the next wave.

I turned to the credenza and its lower drawer, which was heavy with family photos. Shoeboxes full on the bottom, envelopes of photos layered over them, loose prints on top—hundreds of family photos (prints versus slides—add to list). Lifting the top layers, I went to the first shoebox (they were all dated). The color in the photos was faded. My father had way more hair, my mother more of a figure. Okay, breasts. Breasts like Cassie's. She was really very beautiful then.

I lay back on the floor, stared up at the vaulted ceiling.

I got up. In the hallway I hesitated, then turned toward my parents' bedroom.

I stepped inside.

It was big and very pale. They each had a closet, a chest

of drawers, a nightstand. First I looked in my mother's closet. Her clothes, arranged in order from informal to formal wear, were long on business suits and blazers. Way to the side, almost unreachable behind the door, were some older sleeveless tops. Very summery, very seventies.

In her chest of drawers were her stockings, bras, and panties. I didn't take them out; she would know, and besides, I'm not a pervert. They were nice bras and panties, however; some were semi-see-through, and the newer panties looked high cut. Weird Thought of the Day: She could wear those. She does, idiot, another voice in my head replied.

I turned to her nightstand. Mainly books by women authors and some law reviews. Some lotion, including a small purple jar of "Total Body Massage" moisturizer. Some old earrings, a new box of earplugs (my father snores), a nail clipper, a narrow velvet pouch. I opened the little sack. "Personal Massager," the inside flap read. The smooth little plastic tube had an on-off switch; I touched it. The device buzzed like a snake in my hand. Yikes! I turned it off and put it back exactly where it was. So much for snooping on your parents—you find out things you don't want to know, and it serves you right.

My father's closet doors unfolded to his smell: September leaves and firewood. His sport coats, all one of them (he was wearing the other), were brown and gray with matching elbow patches. Lots of long-sleeved crews and turtlenecks. Even more flannel shirts: a dozen or more, all earth tones with a couple of reds for color. Khakis, a half dozen pair. Lots of sweaters, wool and cotton. I held up a blue sweater; I could wear this. It would fit. At the far end of the closet, with dust on the shoulders, I spotted two more sport coats with wide lapels, real stylin'——for twenty years ago.

His socks and underwear drawers were a mess. His underwear consisted of a corner jammed with old briefs, JCPenney brand, but all his recent shorts were boxers. I recognized them from the laundry. We both wore boxers.

His nightstand drawer was heavy with stuff, a real junk drawer. *Men's Journals*, *Log Home Living*, a thin and hardbound *Book of Proverbs*. I opened the Bible volume and the spine crackled; my father was not much for church or religion. Digging deeper, I found a duck call, a magnetic compass, pencil stubs, dozens of matchbooks from motels and restaurants in Minnesota and Wisconsin. Including one from Ely, The Paddle Inn.

I went back to my room.

I lay on my bed.

But couldn't stop thinking.

After a while I got up and headed downstairs to my father's office. It was a scatter of rough drawings, blueprints, building codes, T squares. One set of prints was pinned open on his drafting board. I glanced down at the corner. The address was 200 South Pioneer Road (Shagawa Lake), Ely, Minnesota. Canoe country. There was no owner name, which seemed odd.

I looked over the pages. It was a timber frame home with a large fireplace and vaulted roof with skylights. I turned to other pages: more of the same—the second floor, the balconies, the screened porch, and so on. The last, bottom, page was the topographical map, which showed elevation and proximity to the lake. I thought of the blond woman. The blue water behind her.

Back in my room, I called up Gertrude's photos on the screen. Though the photo was cropped, I could see the lake, a far horizon of trees, and something small and white—possibly a house or shed. That was all.

I thought about things for a long time, then punched up Gertrude's address. I wrote,

Why are you doing this to me?
Jed

I got back a message within a minute.

Because he's your father, plus an asshole besides, and I already have one of those.
Gertrude

I replied:

Have what? father or asshole? or asshole father? You have
pronoun reference problems. And BTW, do you do instant
messaging? We could talk better.
Jed

She made me wait five minutes. On purpose, I guessed.

I don't do IM--I have a life. And you think this is all freaking
funny?
Gertrude

I replied.

Sorry. This will work fine. But what do you want from me anyway?
Jed

I had to wait several more minutes this time.

I want you to make your father leave us alone. And if he doesn't,
I know where your mother works (the law office on 8th Street).
I know where you go to church (Methodist on 2nd Ave). I know
where your sisters go to college (University of Minnesota).
I know everything about your family. So imagine if some pix
of the happy couple showed up everywhere in your town.
Attachment (if you dare).
Gert

My heartbeat started doing its weird dance again. I waited several long seconds before clicking on the attachment. I placed the cursor on "Stop" and got ready to click it just in case my brain couldn't take the whole photo.

The image inched downward. Blue sky, green trees replacing black. It was a forest, major pine trees. The pointy top of a green tent. To the side, my father and the blond woman. The photo was taken through branches and tall grass, as if the photographer were lying on the ground. As were my father and the blonde. He was kissing her and her neck was arched and it was clear that they were both naked. Her shoulders were really large. I hit STOP before the photo reached the small of my father's back. Before things went any further. I could look at the image only from the very side of my eye. Then I punched the monitor's power button; the image sizzled to to black.

I got back into bed.

I lay there. In the dark, my computer's little green sleep light blinked in a slow, steady rhythm. If I squinted, it was the tiny light on a big ore freighter far out on Lake Superior at night. One of those long, rusty ships with an unpronounceable foreign name, heading into deeper and deeper water.

CHAPTER FIVE

At breakfast my mother said to me cheerfully, "I see you were looking through the family photos."

Damn. I had forgotten to put them away.

"Find any ones in particular? I noticed you left out some old ones of your father and me."

"Yeah. Well. Actually, there's this school project. Part of history class—personal history, it's called. We're supposed to do some research on our own families," I said, improvising, snatching at ideas. I realized that lying was something I'd always been good at.

"Like a family tree or something?" my father asked without looking up from the paper.

"Sort of," I said.

"Interesting," my mother replied. She turned away. As I watched her move across the kitchen, I flashed on her family, how she never saw much of them.

"But more focused on our own parents," I added. "Their backgrounds, how they met, their jobs, that sort of thing." I shrugged as if it were just another boring assignment and bent to my cereal.

"There's Take Your Daughter To Work Day, so why not Take Your Son To Work Day?" my father said, turning to my mother. He said this as if my mother's were the real job in the family.

"You're very welcome to come along sometime," she said to me.

"Great," I answered, "but first we're supposed to start with the father." I turned to him. "In fact, if you go up to Ely on Friday, maybe I could come along?"

There was silence. My father kept looking at the newspaper; however, his eyes stopped moving along the newsprint.

"Garrett? Did you hear Jeddy?"

"Friday? Come along to Ely?" He blinked as if he had been reading, or at least thinking of something else. I could guess what; suddenly I hated him. "I suppose," he said. "It'll be a long and boring day, but if you really want to come, sure that's fine. Sure."

"Great," I said, and faked a smile.

"I do have other projects closer to home," he said, looking straight at me. "You wouldn't have to miss a full day of school."

"I certainly don't mind," I answered (my mother laughed at that), and I manufactured a smile—as if life were good.

After school I checked my e-mail. Something from Gertrude was there.

J—
Well, what are you doing about *our* problem?
Gert

I shot a note back.

I'm waiting for the right moment to talk to him.
J

I got her answer:

"Right moment"--how sweet. There is no right moment, idiot.
But just to show you I'm not cruel, I'll give you seven days.
After that, bad news starts to rain on Duluth like seagull shit.
And here's another incentive: If your father stops seeing my
mother, this all goes away quietly. Nobody else finds out.
Especially your mother.
Ger

I thought about this for a minute, then typed:

Does your mother know that you know? About my father, I mean?
J

I heard back quickly:

Sure she knows. And she doesn't care if I do. She's a real slut, and she's drunk most of the time--but I'm all she's got. I take care of her mostly. Unless you'd like to.
G

I tried to imagine a family like hers. They must be real losers. She didn't say anything about a father. He was probably long gone. I imagined Gertrude and her mother living in some dump of a trailer house with railroad tracks on one side and a swamp full of mosquitoes on the other. But that didn't square with the new lake house under construction. Lots of things didn't add up.

No thanks, got a mother. My plan right now is to talk to my father on Friday, and then this will be over and we can all move on.
J

I waited.

Maybe over for you, Preppy. Me, I'll just have to do this again in a few months with another psycho. Like I said, she's a real slut. She's been in and out of rehab for years. But when it comes to parents, we take what we get, yes? You just do your thing on Friday and don't bother me until it's done. To make sure you stay on task, look for some more photos next week. I'll try not to disgust you.

I let out a breath, but my heart still pounded. To relax, I bailed out of my e-mail and checked the Major League baseball scores, checked the weather radar (nothing cooking), checked the live cam on Bourbon Street in New Orleans (the usual drunks), and then went looking for Alyssa Milano. Nothing new there, either, so I went to www.coeds-tanning.com and looked at the girls, at their thong bikinis, at the blue ocean behind. I took a similar link to www.free-beaches.com, and then another and another. Later my eyes started to burn, and I looked up: It was 3:00 A.M.

On Friday morning our father-son trip began. My father and me in his Ford Explorer headed up Highway 61 as if life were good. He had his blueprints, cell phone, camera, binoculars, fifty-foot tape measures—all the usual gear.

"Well, this is different," my father began. He flashed a smile.

"I hope I won't get in the way."

"No, no problem," he said.

We rode along through the northern part of Duluth; cars streamed into the city, carrying people to offices downtown.

"Me, I could never do the eight to five," my father said.

"Like Mom?" I said.

He glanced at me, then back to the road. "She works hard." It was like he wanted to say more—more about her, more about them—but he didn't. I said nothing, and we rode along, putting the city behind us.

The road proceeded northeast straight along Lake Superior. On my side, the cliffs dropped away and the water glinted cold and dark. Here and there, a leftover floe of pale ice still drifted. A gray ore freighter, out farther still and tiny as a sliver of wood, crawled away east, toward the other Great Lakes and eventually salt water.

"Looks cold out there," my father said.

I nodded. *Say, Dad? There's something I need to talk to you about. . . .* But I couldn't do it. Soon. Later for sure. But not right now. We rode on in silence.

After about a half hour we reached Two Harbors, then turned north. Highway 2 cut like a laser line through the heavy pines and impenetrable swamps of the Finland State Forest, which was part of the Superior National Forest. On higher ground were Norway pines nearly the size of small redwood trees. The lower ground cupped bogs and gnarly cedar swamps. Looking out into the bush, I thought of Goodman Brown's forest. *Was it real or was it a dream?*

"Keep your eyes peeled; I've seen moose in this area. Eagles, too," he said.

I nodded. *Say, Dad? There's something I need to . . .*

After an hour we turned left onto Highway 1, which was winding, plus heaved in spots from the winter frost going out. Trees leaned closer to both sides of the road. Ahead, crows clustered on the brown splatter of a road-kill deer; as we drew even, they flapped away. We drove on, past low gray fingers of rock that bent the road gently side to side. The rock fingers turned to knuckles, the knuckles to car-size fists of stone furred with moss and scrubby fir trees rising from their crevices. It was the beginning of the Canadian Shield. Small lakes glinted brightly through the trees, and "BWCAW" signs started to appear. We were close to the Boundary Waters Canoe Area Wilderness, and to Ely, the last major outpost.

"Be a good time to be on the lake with a paddle," my father said. "A little chilly but probably too early for the blackflies."

"Don't remind me," I replied.

He smiled.

We were referring to a family trip a few years ago—one of the few we've taken, it occurred to me—with my two sisters, two canoes, and the blackfly hatch of the century, not to mention a major thunderstorm that soaked our gear. But the flies were worst. They weaseled inside our collars, our ears, up our noses—and bit like crazy. When we got home, my whole family looked like we had acne. We could have scored an Accutane commercial and made big money.

"That trip is the reason your mother won't go paddling with me anymore," he said, still smiling, though not so broadly.

"Hey, the flies and the weather were brutal," I added. "I was what, only six or seven?"

"Six. And yeah, it was bad," he said. We drove on a bit. "But maybe that's why it's a wilderness area. Nature's way of keeping people at bay."

"Could be," I offered. All in all, a satisfactory conversation. *Say, Dad? There's something . . .*

We drove on past curving, rocky shorelines. Little lakes and bogs. Over the Isabella River, and on through the woods. My father hummed lightly to himself; he seemed relaxed by this wild country. He understood nature and was at home with it. Me, I had gotten good in a canoe, but I liked my out-of-doors in small doses. A weekend paddle here, a day trip there. I sometimes thought my father could live out of a canoe and tent.

Say, Dad? There's . . .

We passed the road to White Iron Lake. Not far beyond, just south of Ely, a rusted iron-ore conveyer jutted from a hill like a giant, ancient ski jump. This was the edge of the iron-mining Mesabi Range. I waited for my father to announce this. But he didn't.

"Ely," he said as we arrived at the city limits.

I watched the sign pass: ELY: POPULATION 3,916.

We turned on the main street, Sheridan Avenue, and headed through town. It was as hilly as Duluth, and every other business looked to be a canoe outfitter or Boundary Waters souvenir–type store. On the left was The Paddle Inn. I watched my father's eyes; their gaze flickered sideways, but not long enough for me to deduce anything. We turned north at the Chocolate Moose Restaurant. I looked back; I kept close track of our turns.

"We're headed north of town, to Shagawa Lake," my father said.

I nodded. We passed more giant, rusted mining towers and their lifts and cables; past a small Holiday Inn; and then along Shagawa Lake. It was a typical Canadian Shield–type lake: curving bays, little islands here and there bristled with dark spruce and pines. Soon we we turned left onto a bumpy gravel road, and then left again onto a narrow driveway newly slashed through the pines. The driveway curved downward toward flashes of blue water. I thought of the blond woman; her wide shoulders.

"I've got a really nice lake place going up here," he said, already rustling open his blueprints as he drove. "The owners had read one of my articles on lakeshore building, and that's how we got hooked up."

Say, Dad?

We stopped beside some tradesmen's pickups with lettering on their doors and sawhorses and tools in the rear. A log home with a soaring peak, roofed but without doors and windows yet, overlooked the lake. Across, nearly a mile on the opposite shore, was a tiny white boathouse. My stomach flip-flopped.

"Great view," I managed to say.

"Yes," he replied, smiling as he stared toward the lake. "I just love this site."

I'll bet you do.

"So who's the owner?" I asked, pretending interest in the house.

"A family from Ely," he said; he rustled open more blueprints.

"Say, Dad," I began. My heart slammed loudly in my ears.

"Dammit," he said; he took a closer look at the actual roof.

"What?" I said.

"Just as I thought. No skylights." He let out a long, annoyed breath, then gathered up his blueprints. "Welcome to my world, son."

We got out. The air was fresh and early-May warm and smelled of newly cut pine boards. Pounding came from inside the house.

"Architects and builders are like cats and dogs," my father said. "It's just the way it is in the building trades."

I nodded.

"Morning, gents!" my father called to the carpenters.

"Hey," the nearest tradesman grunted coolly.

"Morning," said another, an older man; he only briefly looked our way.

"Dale, I brought my son along today. Jed, I'd like you meet one of the best builders in northern Minnesota."

The man turned. He had a ruddy, not unkindly face; he stuck out a thick, chapped hand. "Dale Jenkins. Howdy."

"Jed Berg," I said.

The older man's eyes narrowed. "You ain't thinking of becoming an architect like your old man, I hope?" Above on the scaffolding, the carpenters guffawed.

"Not sure yet," I said.

"Actually he's thinking of going into skylight design," my father said.

"The kind that don't leak?" Mr. Jenkins said.

There was laughter from above.

"I think I'm in the middle of something here," I said.

Mr. Jenkins smiled pleasantly. "Sorry, son. Your dad and I disagree once in a while, that's all."

I hung around while the two men discussed things, then followed my father back to our truck. He spread the blueprints over the hood and took out his cell phone. "I need to call the owners," he said.

I nodded. I didn't move.

"This might take me a while. You're welcome to wander around."

"Sure, okay," I said.

As I walked away, he was poring over the blueprints; only after I was out of earshot did he pick up the telephone.

With binoculars from the truck, I went down by the shore. An older Grumman canoe lay on the bank. The Canadian Shield rock was stained brown, and the water lapping at it was coffee dark. A loon let out a brief "hahahaha" far out on the lake. Yeah, real funny.

Looking over my shoulder to make sure my father was occupied, I slipped from my shirt pocket a printout of the photo of him and the blond woman. I looked down, then up. I trained the binoculars across the lake. White and square, right on the waterline. I looked around, then down at the muddy, rocky ground; in the first photo, they had to have been standing right here.

I felt a little bit dizzy; I moved away a few yards.

And the other photos, the ones in the woods, with the tent? I looked toward the trees; there was forest all around. A faint game trail ran along the shore and into the woods. I followed it. Just out of sight from the house, a few yards off the trail, I saw a small natural opening. Moss and pine needles were flattened in a square shape. The footprint of a tent. That throw-uppy, nauseous feeling hit me again—that and a couple of blackflies. I retreated.

Back at the shore, I sat in the breeze on a large stone for

a while, getting my breath, pretending to scan the lake with the binoculars. I started to get this strange, now-or-never feeling. This overwhelming urge to blurt out everything. Just get it over with.

I headed quickly back to the truck. As I came up behind my father, he was saying, "I'm not sure that's a good idea." At that moment, my tennis shoes crunched on gravel: He looked around.

"But if you think so, okay," he added, nodding at me. I'd swear there was a change in his voice, a new and fake tone. After a few more generic sentences, he hung up.

Say, Dad? "Say, Dad?"

He frowned. "The owner is wavering on these skylights, no thanks to you-know-who," he said, with a nod toward the house and Mr. Jenkins.

"Listen, Dad—"

"The owners are coming out from town."

"They're coming here?" I said.

He nodded.

"Right now?"

"Yes." He turned to me; there was an odd look in his eyes.

"Will I, like, be in the way?" I said. I was chickening out fast.

He swallowed. "You really don't have to hang around at all. In fact, there's a canoe and paddle down by the shore."

"I don't mind. It's why I came, really," I said. I had managed to get back some of my courage; I just wanted to see her, even from a distance. I just wanted to know what she really looked like.

"Okay, suit yourself," he murmured.

Only a few minutes later, two vehicles came down the driveway. A pickup with MARVIN WINDOWS lettered on the side followed a newer, dark Jeep Cherokee. Out of the driver's side of the Jeep stepped a short, middle-size man, and from the other side came the large blond woman. She was a totally plain woman who was nearly the same height and weight as my father. I froze; it was as if blood stopped moving in my veins. A bimbo or a college-girl intern was explainable, but not this woman.

"Well, back to work," my father said to me. His voice sounded odd, but maybe it was my ears shutting down. Like the rest of me.

I pretended to yawn. "Maybe I will take a little paddle in the canoe," I said. "I'm getting the drift of things here."

"Sure, Jeddy, fine," he said quickly. "Go ahead. And take your time, son."

Son. God I hated this day.

I headed down to the canoe. He didn't even remind me to wear a life jacket.

CHAPTER SIX

When I paddled back, nearly an hour later, the sun was higher and blackflies greeted me at the shore. But the owners' Jeep was gone; I peeked around some rocks to make sure. On the roof, men were sawing square holes for the skylights. My father and the window representative stood high up on the hip roof near the workmen; Mr. Jenkins remained on the ground, his arms folded as he watched.

He turned to me as I came up behind him. "Well, Jed, you get bored and take a little paddle?" I got the feeling he preferred not to watch holes being cut in his roof.

"Yes. It's a nice lake," I said.

"Sure is." He looked across the water for a long moment. "Trouble with my job is, I got to work all summer. Hardly have time to pick up my fishing rod, let alone a canoe paddle. It's only the tourists who get to enjoy this country."

He turned back to watch the men work.

"But it's a beautiful house," I observed.

"That it is, son." He turned and gave me a trace of a smile.

"Your father's pretty good at what he does."

"Who owns it?" I asked. I dropped my volume slightly.

"Family in Ely. The Sanborns. A doctor and teacher. Guess it's gonna be their second place. I don't ask, I just build 'em." He called out something to a carpenter and stepped forward to give further directions. I moved off to the side, pretended to inspect the log corners of the house.

We were on the road back to Duluth by two o'clock. It was clear there would have been no reason for my father to stay overnight in Ely. No work-related reason, that was.

"Well, Jeddy," he said, "did you learn anything today?" Now that we were leaving, he was lively and pleased. He had an air about him of just having dodged a bullet. Avoided a falling tree. Swerved to miss a deer on the highway. Gotten himself safely back on the straight and narrow with no harm done.

Well, let's see . . . I saw the plain Jane you're sleeping with. "I guess so," I mumbled.

"Like what?"

"Well, the positioning of the house. The winter sunlight thing."

He smiled. "By the way, you were helpful with that sky-light discussion. A good icebreaker with old Dale. Hell, I ought to bring you more often." He chuckled and turned up the music. We drove along in silence.

"So is that a year-round home or a summer place or what?" I asked.

"Could be either," he said. He glanced sideways at me. We rode along in silence.

"Hey, what say we stop and get us a late lunch?"

"Sure," I said. I could use something to eat; I realized I had put on several miles in that canoe.

We stopped in Ely, which was rather ballsy of him, I thought, at the Minglewood Café. There, at a huge half-log bar, we ordered burger basket combos with large fries. There was country music on the radio, and a mix of locals and "Kevlar couples," as my father called them—upscale canoeists from Minneapolis and beyond.

One such couple sat just two stools away. My father nodded to the younger fellow and his wife, who were wearing fresh Cabela and REI outdoor shirts and hats. They were eating a huge lunch.

"You folks coming or going?" my father asked.

"Going in today," the man said, with a glance to his wife. "Last good meal for a week." He laughed.

His wife, who did not look like the outdoors type—she was fine boned like my mother—managed a small smile.

"What's the blackfly report?" my father asked.

"Blackflies?" the man said; his wife looked at him.

"Early May now, looks like the first hatch," my father said

pleasantly. "They can get a little bothersome. It's good to have bug spray along, maybe even head nets."

"Head nets?" the woman asked

"Kind of like beekeepers wear," my father explained. "They're inexpensive. Any of the local outfitters would have them."

The man shrugged and kept eating.

"We do have some mosquito spray," the woman said. She looked at her husband. "Don't we?"

The husband laughed. "The flies can't be that bad."

"Usually they're not," my father replied.

"I'm sure we'll be fine," the husband said to his wife, taking charge, turning away from us now. His wife looked at him uncertainly.

"Have a good paddle," my father said. He swiveled back to me with the smallest of shrugs. I returned to my food.

"'They can't be that bad,'" my father whispered, imitating the man's voice.

"We do have some mosquito spray—don't we?" I added.

I tucked down my head and managed to disguise my laughter with a brief coughing fit. I almost blew Pepsi out my nose; so far, it was the best moment of the trip.

My father and I got a grip and kept working on our burgers. The Kevlar couple finished up and seemed to be unhappy when they left. The husband shot us an annoyed look as he went out the door.

We laughed for real this time.

Then he said, "Listen, Jeddy, I should make one last call to that homeowner. Keep eating, son. I'll be right back."

So much for great father-and-son moments.

"Construction details, they'll kill you," he added with his false voice.

My throat started to close up as I watched him go. I had trouble swallowing, so I made myself eat slowly. Before he returned, my French fries were cold and clammy.

"Sorry to take so long," he said easily. "But I got things squared away."

"Sure, Dad," I said. For something to do, I kept eating the last of my cold, limp fries.

We finally left the café. In the parking lot, I said suddenly, "Wait up. I forgot my sunglasses—I'll be right back."

Just inside the door I turned to the tattered phone book, looked rapidly under S. Two Sanborns. One was a rural route address, one was in town. The local one also had a children's line. Number 680 James Street, Donald and Sarah Sanborn, plus the phone numbers. I peeked through the small foyer window toward the parking lot. My father waited in the SUV. I slipped in the coins and dialed the in-town Sanborns.

"Sanborns," a woman's voice said almost immediately. She

did not sound like a drunk or a slut.

I held my breath.

"Hello?" she said expectantly. "Hello?" She lowered her voice. "Gary?"

I put the receiver back. It weighed a hundred pounds. I almost threw up right there in the booth.

We drove south and I pretended to doze. But gradually I started to sit up straighter and straighter. "Can we stop at a gas station?"

"Well, there aren't many along here."

"Like soon," I added.

"Feeling okay? You look a little white."

"I'm not sure about those fries."

"I hear you."

We drove along. I started to feel my food higher up in my stomach, then in my throat. "Anywhere is fine. Maybe just pull over now?" I breathed. I felt clammy and sweaty, too.

Quickly my father found the shoulder and braked to stop. I barely threw open the door before I spewed.

"Sorry," I gasped.

"Hey, it's okay. The road is kind of up and down from frost heaves; maybe I was hurrying a bit."

I let out one smaller after-spew, then took a drink of bottled water that my father offered, and spit.

"Feel better?"

"Kind of," I said.

"I'll take it slower the rest of the way. This Highway One is brutal," he said as we pulled back onto the asphalt.

I didn't want to talk. I lay over in the seat and closed my eyes. After a while I felt his hand and arm resting on my back. I felt too shitty to object, so I let it ride. It felt like when I was kid. When life was good.

As we entered Duluth, I was sitting up. I had drunk a couple of colas and was completely over my nausea. "That was strange back there," I said.

"Touch of car sickness. All you kids had it," my father answered.

We looked down at the Lift Bridge, silvery in the late sunlight.

"I never take for granted how pretty it is here," my father said.

Say, Dad? There's something we really need to—But we were too close to home now. I had failed.

My mother was happy to see us. "How was take-your-kid-to-work day?" she asked.

"Successful, I'd say, yes, son?"

"Sure, you bet," I said as we went inside.

"There's some leftover Chinese on the counter if you're

hungry," my mother said.

"No thanks," I answered quickly. My father smiled at me; he said nothing about my car sickness.

"I think I'll just turn in," I said. "I'm really beat."

"Tough day on the job!" My mother smiled too.

"I'll take school any day," I said in parting. My parents laughed as I headed up the stairs.

Just before I closed my door, I hear my mother say softly, "Well—a Friday evening free."

His reply, which I couldn't hear, made her laugh. There was some murmuring. Then silence. Then another chuckle. I felt a rush of nausea at their sounds. For God's sakes, they were going to make love. I closed my door and braced against it while I got my breath. Then I lay down on my bed. Across the room, the green sleep light blinked on my computer. I thought about things for a long time, then rose and woke up my Mac.

Dear Gertrude--
Major new developments. I've got to talk to you. Can we meet at Perkins again?
Say next week sometime?
J

I waited for her reply, which came soon.

Okay, but you'd better have good news; Monday at 5:30 p.m. will work.
G.

I looked at her writing. At the punctuation. Not a lot of punk chicks knew or cared about the semicolon. But I was too tired to think anymore. I lay in my dim room watching that tiny, blinking green light.

CHAPTER SEVEN

On Monday I made sure to get to Perkins early. I didn't go in but hung in the parking lot in the car and watched the front door.

At five P.M. the usual crowd of students began to disperse. As they were leaving, a flash of pink caught my eye. The punk chick slipped around the side of the restaurant; she must have walked from somewhere or else parked in the rear. She was carrying a weathered Duluth pack. I waited another five minutes, then headed inside.

The place was still semibusy with the after-school crowd.

"One or two?" the hostess said tiredly, holding a menu.

"I'm meeting someone. Girl with the pink hair?"

"Ain't she cute," the woman said flatly. She turned; I followed.

At the booth, Gertrude looked up at me. "Well, well, preppy. You're early."

"You too," I said.

She popped her gum nastylike as she stared at me. "So, what's the good news?"

"Actually, I thought maybe we should start by getting to know each other better. It might help us, you know, get things worked out."

She snapped her gum in one loud pop. "In other words, you haven't told him."

I shrugged. "I've been sick. As a dog. In bed for two days." This much at least was true. Something about that trip gave me a fever and chills, and I couldn't stop sleeping.

"What a loser you are." She chomped her gum and glared at me.

"Thank you so much," I said. *Tell me, have your parents always driven a Jeep? Do you like living on James Street?*

"So what are we here to talk about?" she said.

"Well," I began, "I was thinking that the more I know about what my old man's been up to, the more, like, cards I have to play when I talk to him."

"Talk to him when?" she said sarcastically. "It better be soon. Tick-tock."

I ignored that. "I mean, how did this thing between them start? How long has it been going on?"

She shrugged. "I don't know how it started. I suppose they met in some bar."

"My father doesn't drink."

Her eyes flickered past mine to the door, to the parking lot beyond. "Don't ask me. I just know they sneak around and screw like rabbits."

I flinched.

"What—can't take the truth?" she said.

"You don't have to be crude."

"Hey, I'm way less crude than those two."

I glanced up at the waitress, who had suddenly appeared with pencil poised.

"A milk shake, I guess. Chocolate." I turned to Gertrude. "You want something?"

"No," she said, and popped her gum at the waitress, who turned on her heel.

I looked to Gertrude. "So, you sneak around and take photos of them?"

She stared. "A picture is worth a thousand words, right?"

"You're kind of literary at times," I said. "You use good punctuation, too."

Her eyes narrowed with anger. "So you gonna talk to your old man or not?"

"Yes. I'm working on it."

"Well, work harder, dammit."

I looked her up and down. "If your mother does this all the time, I mean, gets drunk and acts like a slut, why are you making such a big deal about my father?" I watched her face closely.

She swallowed. "I don't like any of the men she sleeps

with, but I like him less," she said. "He's a creep."

"Actually he's a pretty good father," I said.

"But a piss-poor husband."

"Listen, dammit, he might be a cheat but——"

"But what, preppy!" she said. People turned our way at our loud voices, and just then the waitress appeared with my milk shake.

I took it in silence. I bent my head and sipped the shake.

When I looked up, Gertrude was staring at the shake; I got the feeling she was hungry, but I sure as hell wasn't going to share.

"Anyway, where were we?" I said.

She shrugged. "I forget."

I kept sipping my shake. "Do you go to school or what?"

"You don't need to know."

"Do you have a father? Any sisters or brothers?"

"You don't need to know."

"Live around here?" *Like in Ely?*

"You for sure don't need to know that."

"Okay, okay. So I guess there's not much to talk about," I said, working deeper into the shake. Her eyes followed my straw. "I just wanted to meet today and tell you I'm making progress and that this is all going to work out."

"It better," she muttered.

We sat there in silence as I finished my shake. I loudly

rattled up the last of it through my straw. "Well, I guess I'll take off," I said, reaching for the check.

"You do that, preppy," she said, popping her gum.

"See you."

"I hope not."

I shrugged.

"Tick-tock," she called. "Seagulls are circling your house."

"Sort of like that Hitchcock movie?"

"Worse," she said.

I walked away.

In the parking lot I made a show of unlocking the car, adjusting the mirror, then driving off. From the corner of my eye I saw her pink hair inside the restaurant; she was watching me. I drove around the block, then parked where I could see through the restaurant windows.

Waited for twenty minutes.

I saw the waitress come back and eventually bring a major tray of food. Gertrude wolfed it down, then finally got up to leave. I wondered if she left a tip. Probably not.

Finally she came out. She glanced around, then slipped into her car, a small blue Chevy, and headed out. I let her go a block, then followed well back in traffic. She wasn't hard to trail—her pink hair stood out among the other drivers—and anyway, I was pretty sure which way she would turn.

Left now, north onto Highway 61, the road to Ely. "Gotcha!" I muttered.

I slowed by the Glensheen Mansion and prepared to turn back to Duluth—which is when her pink hair came off. One moment it was there, the next moment gone. I blinked, straightened, leaned forward for a better look; then I swerved back behind her (three cars) just to make sure I wasn't dreaming. Sure enough, no pink hair, just a blond ponytail she had pulled up tight like every other girl in high school.

After a few blocks her Chevy's brake lights came on and she pulled into a Quik-Stop gas station. Hurriedly she parked, then went inside carrying a gym bag; I parked and watched, tracking her progress down the aisles of chips and candy. She disappeared into the women's room. I slouched down in the car seat and waited.

In a couple of minutes she came out: sweats and ponytail and scrubbed face—no black makeup or metal piercings.

"Double gotcha!" I muttered. "Gertrude" Sanborn, ex-punk chick, got in her little blue Chevy. Through my mirror I watched her drive off; watched her car blend in with traffic and disappear.

Toward Ely.

A nice small town.

One I planned to visit again real soon.

CHAPTER EIGHT

I went back to Perkins and found Derek Jones from my English class. "Can I talk to you?" I said.

"You are, man."

"Not here," I said.

"What? Jed-eye Berg doesn't want to be seen talking with Weird Derek?"

I ignored that. "It's a computer question. An . . . access problem; there's a site I need to visit, but there's the little matter of a password."

A gleam came into his black eyes. He shrugged. "Sure. Come by my house."

A half hour later, we sat in Derek's dank, smelly basement bedroom. It was littered with electronic equipment, Fender guitar parts, and adult magazines. I mean, they were just lying around, *Playboy*, *Penthouse*, *Hustler*, you name it. He noticed me looking.

"Sometimes I get tired of Internet porn, you know what I mean?"

"Sure," I said. I managed a lame chuckle, then ignored the skin mags.

I watched Derek's fingers rattle the keyboard of his PC. Off to the side was a jumble of gaming equipment. No wonder he slept through most of his classes. I continued to watch Derek, but he lost me after about five moves. "Rock 'n' roll," he said, peering at his screen. "Ely High School."

A couple more strokes. "Here she is: Laura Sanborn."

I leaned forward to the glowing screen.

"What do you want to know about her?" Derek asked.

"Everything."

He clattered keys for a couple of minutes, then his printer began to whir with sheets of data. Laura Sanborn, age seventeen, junior at Ely High. Birth date, Social Security number, grade point average (4.0), extracurricular activities (debate, tennis, choir, band, mock trial, cross-country ski team, Junior Olympics kayak team), it was all there—even her class schedule, hour by hour, at Ely High.

"She also owes $2.50 to the cafeteria lady and has one overdue book," Derek added.

"Sweet," I said as I scanned through the printouts.

"Piece of cake, man," he said.

Then I didn't know quite what to say. I didn't want to hang around Derek's moldy basement bedroom. I said, "Hey, thanks, man."

"No problem."

There was silence.

"Can I like pay you or something?"

He stared at me. "Pay me?" he said. "Pay me? This ain't some stupid freaking job." He sounded suddenly all pissed off. He turned to his computer screen and wouldn't speak or even look at me again. Finally I left. I just don't understand some people.

Tuesday I skipped school. Tuesday was perfect. No crimes, nothing interesting ever happens on a Tuesday. Check the police reports, the accident statistics, and you'll see: Tuesday is the best day of all to try something shady. Bobby was waiting in the school parking lot with his Domino's gear.

"Can't you at least tell me where you're going?" Bobby whined, holding back the stuff.

"Top secret—but I'll tell you if I get lucky," I said, gesturing for the bag. I'd told him only that there was a girl involved, which was true.

"You mean there's a chance?" Bobby said, eyes widening. "Like all the way with Cassie?"

"I didn't say Cassie," I said.

"Geez!" Bobby breathed.

I leaned closer, looked briefly about. "She's older. Possibly even married. I'll tell you everything when I get back—before school's out."

"Wow," he said. "That's even better than my family."

I didn't ask him which family, though I could guess; never encourage gamers to talk about their little people.

"Anyway, here's the stuff." He held out the bag.

"Thanks. It's the perfect disguise."

"But don't lose anything, especially the roof sign," Bobby said. "They make us pay for them."

"Hey, you know me, I'm dependable."

Bobby shrugged. Said nothing. I guess I had stiffed him more than once—but only on small stuff, like saying I would pick him up and then not showing. Little things like that.

"Remember, every detail," he said.

"High school junior tells all," I promised, turning away.

As I drove west out of town, my heart did the funny dance again, like my chest was too small and my heart was banging against my rib cage. But my skip day was totally covered. Students at my school were divided into "good kids" and "bad kids," and everybody pretty much knew which group they belonged to. Since I was a "good kid," it was easier to lie to my teachers. As well, this morning I disguised my voice and called in my absence to the attendance hot line. And lastly, my mother and father (luckily) were to be gone all day. I liked how everything was in order, everything in its place. Maybe I had more of my mother's personality than I admitted.

The car ran smoothly as I headed north from the city (I had made sure to have a full tank of gas). Soon the highway became two-lane blacktop with water in the ditches. The water looked cold, and deep in spots. An eagle sat hunched in a tree: There was probably a dead deer nearby. I watched my driving, my speed; this was the kind of road, with forest close on both sides, where you had to pay attention. Where you actually had to drive. It was the same road my father and I had taken, but this trip felt totally different. I began to think dark, Hawthorneian thoughts—like all the things that could go wrong with the Honda.

A broken fan belt.

A flat tire.

An overheated radiator.

But nothing at at all went wrong.

At the outskirts of Ely, I stopped at the tourist information center and called the Sanborn house. The leave-your-message was Laura's voice—the cheerful Laura, not the angry punk Laura.

"Nobody home, thank you," I said to myself. Back in the car, I slipped into my disguise: my favorite hooded sweatshirt, a Domino's pizza cap, sunglasses, and a Domino's delivery cone for the roof. On the seat, of course, were my "deliveries," a couple of empty cardboard pizza boxes.

Next stop, 680 James Street: the Sanborn house.

It was an older but classy brick house, two stories, shutters, flower beds, big porch with white columns. I circled the block once, then parked, grabbed my empty pizza box, and trotted up to the porch. I rang the doorbell; looked in the windows. There were a grand piano, lots of bookcases, a couple of kayak paddles just inside the front door. For a second I thought I heard noises inside and almost bolted. But then it was quiet. Maybe a pet, or just my paranoia. I glanced both ways, then went along the side of the house. As I came around the corner of the back porch, I froze: A group of three skinny punk kids—two of them older—sat on the wooden porch floor in a circle. Smokers. Seen through the white rails, they looked like they were in jail. Then they heard me. The youngest one, with lime-green hair and very black, raccoon-type eye shadow, scrambled upright. "Shit!" she blurted. The two older girls shrieked, and then all three raced off, bracelets jangling. They darted through the backyard toward the alley.

"Hey!" I called, just for the hell of it. They only ran faster, and quickly were gone behind some houses. A whiff of marijuana remained—as did, on the lawn, a white, fat joint of marijuna—still smoking.

"Well, well, what have we here?" I murmured.

I didn't smoke dope but thought it might come in handy.

Somehow or other. I pinched off its ash and slipped it inside my hooded sweatshirt pocket. Giving the backyard a brief and final inspection (I noticed two kayaks wrapped tightly in tarps), I came back around to the front.

"Hullo?" said a wispy voice from streetside. I looked up to see a little old lady with a little dog on a leash.

"Pizza delivery," I said cheerfully.

"That's odd," she said, looking at me with a puzzled smile.

"1400 James Street? The Smiths?" I said, pretending to check my address.

"Oh no, you must have something wrong," she said.

"Sorry, I'll go back to headquarters and check," I replied.

I waved cheerfully, trotted to my car, and sped off. I kept an eye on the old lady, who remained in my mirror, staring at me. *Hey, I'm just the Domino's guy.* She made me nervous—as if she knew something—but probably it was my imagination.

To relax a bit, I made a loop around town (I still had the sensation that people were staring at me and my car), then drove by the school. It was an older brick building with a new sign out front: HOME OF THE ELY TIMBERWOLVES. In the parking lot I cruised the rows and soon enough found the little blue Chevy, parked close to the front door (which meant she had arrived early—no surprise there). Her car was easy to keep track of: There was a yellow kayak strapped on top. I popped out for a quick look inside in the car. There was the infamous gym bag, along with various sweat gear, books, tennis shoes, and three kayak paddles. I thought of trying the locks and seeing if that pink wig was in the Duluth pack. That, and leaving a cryptic note on the windshield, one that would totally weird her out. But I didn't want to be caught lurking in the parking lot.

I checked my watch, then her class schedule. One half hour to lunch. That gave me just enough time to slip over to the hospital on Conan and Second Street.

It was your basic small-town hospital, yellow brick, three stories. All I needed was a peek at where her dad worked—his wing, his office number, etc. Two could play the I-know-where-you-live-and-where-your-parents-work game. I slipped into my Domino's mode and trotted inside.

In the hallway, nurses and even a patient in a wheelchair paused to stare at me. More paranoia. I stopped at the desk. "Dr. Sanborn's office?"

The receptionist stared at me strangely as well. "Upstairs and to the left. Pediatrics."

"Thank you!" I said, and hustled off. *Gotta fly, I'm the Domino's guy.* I was getting into my character big-time. I took the stairs two at time and soon enough heard babies crying. Just a peek into the area was all I needed.

I paused at the doorway. Just a few paces inside, peering down at a clipboard, dressed in a white coat, was the big blond woman: Dr. Sanborn.

I froze. An instant before she saw me, I turned tail and zipped back down the stairs.

At the front door, an older man in a security guard outfit stepped toward me. "Excuse me, son."

"Yessir?" I said. I had no choice but to halt.

"I got a call here from reception. Said you're delivering a pizza?"

"That's right, sir."

He stared at me, completely puzzled. His little radio crackled. "Hold on just a second, please." He put his hand on my arm as he listened. Then he looked to me.

"They want to know when we got a Domino's in Ely."

I froze. Good God.

"Ah . . . it's brand-new, sir. Actually, in temporary quarters right now. Soon to be built, you know, but we need to get a head start on deliveries."

A group of nurses came walking toward me with enthusiasm. "Hey, Domino's guy! Can we order lunch?"

I split.

Vamoosed.

Hightailed it.

Disappeared.

A few blocks away, on a side street, I stripped myself and car of all pizza icons, then sat inside getting my wits together.

What a freaking idiot. I might as well have been driving around Ely with an I'm-a-spy-from-another-town light flashing on my car. It took me five minutes to stop shaking.

When I had mostly gotten a grip, I eased the car back near the high school and parked. I waited there and tried not to be an idiot again.

At eleven fifty a bell rang. Students began to filter out, at first a trickle, then a stream. It would be just my luck that she was a cafeteria type and ate at school. But then a throng of girls moved toward the parking lot, led by Laura Sanborn herself. In her khaki skirt and tanned legs and bright top and blond hair, she did not much look like a goth chick. Blond on blond. More like the student council prez and homecoming queen. I watched her through my father's binoculars, then drove forward into the lot. Heart pumping hard, I drove almost directly by her. As she chattered with three boys, her eyes were bright and lively; she had great skin and teeth, plus a figure. I'm talking more curves than Highway 61. In the middle of her conversation, her girl friends, laughing, pulled Laura away. "See you at the Moose," Laura called to the boys.

I gave the Chevy some space, then followed it downtown to the Chocolate Moose Restaurant. It was clearly the lunchtime place to be. As schoolkids clustered around the restaurant and outdoor patio, I pulled my cap down low and slunk inside an adjoining outdoor-gear store. I pretended to look at canoe paddles. At maps of the BWCAW. No head nets ("temporarily out of stock"). Through the door, I watched the restaurant patio. There she sat in the sunlight, high school All-American Laura Sanborn, eating and chatting and laughing with her friends as if life were good.

I stuffed my cap in my back pocket, ran my fingers through my hair, and cut through the crowd toward her table. Her back was to me. I stopped directly behind her.

"Hey, Laura," I said loudly.

She turned.

Saw me.

Went white.

"So, are the milk shakes any good here?" I asked.

She tried to speak but couldn't. Her face turned splotchy red. "The milk shakes? Ah, yeah, sure," she mumbled.

"Good," I said. "Next time I'm in town, I'll be sure to have one." With that, I moved on and disappeared into the crowd.

From behind me, I heard alarmed girl voices: "Laura— who was that?"

"Laura—are you all right?"

"Laura—what's wrong?"

Sweet.

On the way back to Duluth, I sang along with the radio and took the curves way too fast, but I was accidentproof, untouchable. Nothing brightens a day like a little revenge.

CHAPTER NINE

When I arrived home, I had mail.

Jed--
I think we need to meet. Tomorrow after school?
The White Pines on Highway 2. It's halfway for both of us.
Laura

After a toss-and-turn night, I got through school the next day, managing to hold off Bobby's interrogation about my mystery trip, and was on the road at 3:15 P.M. I had lied my way out of tennis practice; Coach Thom was not happy. But I couldn't think about that now. I tried to watch my speed limit. And I certainly didn't want get there early.

We arrived at almost exactly the same time; I saw her little Chevy with kayak turn into the picnic area just as I came around a curve. I pulled in and parked a few yards away from her car. Giant pines towered around. For a few seconds both of us remained inside our vehicles. Somebody had to break the ice; I got out.

Then so did she.

We stared at each other, then walked forward. She wore jeans and an Ely Timberwolves sweatshirt; her yellow hair was tied back. We stopped halfway between our cars; the forest around us was bright spring green; a woodpecker drummed nearby.

"Hello, Jed Berg."

"Hey, Laura Sanborn," I said.

We did not shake hands or anything remotely like that. There was a long silence.

"So how did you . . . ?" she began.

"A bunch of little clues," I said. "My father's work stuff, your photos, your disguise. Something about you—the way you talked, the way you wrote. You didn't seem like a true punk chick."

"I never was a good actress," she said.

"Hey, you had me for a while. But when I was following you in my car, I saw you take off the wig."

"Shit," she said. She suddenly scratched her scalp. "The whole time I wore it, it itched like crazy."

"But the anger, that was convincing," I said.

She narrowed her eyes. "The anger is real."

There was more silence. We both looked around. There were several heavy-duty picnic benches with people's names carved on them: MIKE/SALLY FOREVER inside a heart. "You want to sit down?" I said, gesturing to the cleanest bench.

She nodded.

We took opposite ends of a single log plank. We sat so we didn't have to look at each other.

"So now what?" she said.

"I don't know."

The woodpecker drummed again, then went silent.

"Have you told your father?"

"No," I said. "I was close, but I chickened out."

"It's got to be done." The anger came back in her voice.

"Yeah. I know. And very soon. I'm just gonna, like, blurt it out, just do it."

She was silent. "Me too," she said.

I looked directly at her. "Wait a sec: You haven't told your mother that you know?"

She looked down and kicked at a pinecone.

"Are you freaking serious?" I said, my voice rising.

She shrugged.

"Dammit, you told me—"

"I lied, so there!" she said.

We glared at each other, then looked away, into the woods. "Great," I muttered. "You put all this shit on me and you haven't done a damn thing yourself."

"I found out about them, didn't I?"

I was silent. "True," I said. I looked at her.

"What?" she said instantly.

I shrugged and turned away. "I dunno. I keep thinking I should have known. Or maybe I did know and just didn't want to deal with it."

"So you don't care if your parents split up?"

I turned to look at her. "Shut up!" I said. My voice didn't sound like me.

She blinked and drew back. "I'm sorry, Jed. That came out wrong."

"Screw you! Screw all of this." I could feel my eyes burning, and I didn't want her to see them; I stood up and turned to my car.

"Please! Don't go!" Laura said, jumping up. She touched me for the first time—not actually skin to skin, but clutched the back of my jacket. I could feel her holding me in place.

I stared into the woods and blinked and blinked until my eyes were all right, then slumped back down onto the lovers' bench. I hung my head.

"We have to do this, Jed," she said softly. "We have to have this talk."

"I hate this kind of conversation."

"Most boys do," she said, trying for a joke.

"Very funny," I muttered.

We were silent. Then she said, "Anyway, I was there when they met."

I swallowed.

"Your father came to our house to talk about lake-home ideas. Both my parents were there; it was a first-meeting-for-everybody kind of deal. My mother had read an article of your dad's and liked this lake home he had designed. So an appointment was made and he arrived."

I nodded.

"In his flannel shirt, cool floppy little hat, and his blue-prints under his arm," she said sarcastically.

"That's how he always looks," I said sharply; I was not going to take any shit.

She fell silent.

"So not some bar," I pressed, "right? Your own living room."

"Yes. So I lied again, okay?"

"Well, pardon me!" I said sarcastically. My voice echoed angrily among the large pines.

She reached down and picked up the pinecone.

We were silent again.

"Sorry," I said. "I didn't mean to, like, shout at you."

She shrugged. "Believe me, I understand. But we do need to do this—talk, I mean—without screaming at each other."

I nodded my agreement. Which annoyed the hell out of me.

We were silent awhile.

"Anyway," she continued, "I was hanging around the house while they talked about the lake home—which was my own fault, I might add."

"Why is a lake home your fault?"

"I do some kayaking."

"Junior Olympics," I added. "That would be a lot of kayaking."

She turned to me; she stared a long moment. "You're really not that bad a detective."

I almost smiled. If she only knew. "And by the way, where'd you learn all that stuff about me?"

"Sports," she said. "I know a couple of girls from your school."

"Such as?"

"It doesn't matter," she said. "They're in sports."

"What sports?"

"It's doesn't matter."

I was getting angry in a hurry. "So you just called them up and they told you all about me?"

She looked at me. "Unlike boys, girls can compete against each other and still become friends. And besides, they were happy to tell me because they think you're a jerk."

I stared.

"Anyway," she continued, "back to the matter at hand. Because of my kayaking, my parents thought we should be on a lake. They'd always worried about living on a lake when we kids were small, that we'd drown——"

"You have brothers and sisters?"

"One sister, Jenny, in middle school. Eleven, and a real piece of work, believe me."

I thought of the green-haired wild child on the Sanborn back porch. "I've got two older sisters."

"Anne and Melanie," she said, glancing sideways at me.

I shrugged. Why even bother?

She went on. "Shagawa Lake is close to town, plus it's an entrance lake to the BWCAW, so it was a natural choice. My mother found this lakefront lot, started to read articles, and, well, here we are."

The woodpecker drummed farther away now.

"What a freaking mess," she murmured, as if to herself.

"Hey, you can't blame yourself for how adults behave."

She was silent for a moment. "I guess."

"So then what?" I asked. "I mean, when they met." I wanted and did not want to hear more.

"When your father came to the house, the three of them talked and everybody got on really well," she continued. "Your father said all the right things, I guess, just what they wanted to hear——"

"The site on Shagawa, a log home—that's what he does," I said sharply.

Her mouth dropped open for a moment. "Christ, you've been there, too?"

"Great view, though that white boathouse on the far shore is annoying."

She stared at me. "The e-mail photo."

I nodded. "It's the white speck just beneath your mother's chin."

She let out a breath.

"Hey, I would have found out who you were sooner or later."

"I was hoping later," she said.

"So you snuck around taking pictures of them naked," I continued.

She blushed. "I was just trying to get some . . . evidence."

"Which you could use to blackmail my father. Me. My family."

"No. Yes. God, I don't know. I thought the pictures might somehow force them to stop. I just wanted one, you know, compromising photo that day, and suddenly they started—"

"I don't want to hear about it," I said immediately.

"Sure, okay," she said, holding up her hands. "But I'm not a pervert. It was a stupid thing to do, all right?"

We fell silent.

"Back to my father the architect," I said, still annoyed. "He's not a snake-oil salesman. He designs homes like your parents wanted. No wonder they got on well."

"Too well," Laura said.

I waited.

"Right in the middle of their meeting, my father got a phone call. One of his stupid students—they're always calling him at home about their science projects. And he always takes their calls, no matter what. So he left the room."

"And."

"So it's just the two of them—your father and my mother—in the living room. They're sitting side by side looking over house plans, and the articles your dad has written. My mother is getting really excited about the project. And then, slowly, it gets silent. I'm doing my homework in the kitchen by then, and I start to hear this silence. I figure the meeting isn't going well, so I do my cheerful teenager thing and go in there to help out."

She paused.

"Well?"

"I found them just looking into each other's eyes."

I stared off into the forest; I felt short of breath.

"I had this strange feeling I shouldn't interrupt them," she continued, her voice getting thinner and a little shaky. "But then I knew I had to. The whole scene—it was like this snapshot of the future. I saw them as a couple, I saw them driving around in a car, I saw myself visiting them in the new lake place, I saw my sister totally cracked up and crazy in some juvenile home—I kid you not. I saw it all, like some wrinkle in time. It was the weirdest thing. . . ." Her voice broke at the end.

When she finished, the forest went silent, too.

"I'm sorry," I said dumbly.

She shrugged. We were silent.

"Do you think your parents were ever in love?" she asked, turning to me.

"They got married, didn't they?"

"Yes. But are they in love now?"

I paused. It was my turn to reach down and examine a pinecone; it was like a perfect little tree. "I guess. Kind of."

"Kind of? How can you be *kind of* in love?"

"They seem like they're in love. Once in a while," I mumbled. It was hard to explain. "How would I know?" I pitched the pinecone deep into the woods.

"Do they have sex?"

"Christ!" I sputtered. "Of course."

"Hey, I'm just asking."

"Well, do your parents have sex?" I countered.

"I think so. Though maybe not a lot."

I paused. "I think mine do, like at least once a week."

She seemed a bit surprised; she waited for more.

"Once in a while I hear them, you know, when I get home

from something in the evening and they haven't heard me come in. My mother's the loud one; I think sex for her is, like, a major tension release. Sometimes I think they have sex better than they talk." I stopped. I felt cheap talking about them.

Laura was silent. She stared off to the birches. "Do you think your parents were, like, 'made for each other'?"

I stared at two pale birch trees, side by side but separate. "I think they either once were or thought they were."

There was a pause. "Same for my parents," she said.

We were silent.

"Do your parents argue a lot?" she asked.

"Not really," I said. "I mean, not shouting and screaming, anyway. More like the silent kind."

She nodded. "I hate those. I'd rather they had the loud kind."

"So what do your parents disagree on?"

"Not much really. Mainly because my dad never says anything," she said.

I waited.

She went on. "He has this logical, scientific kind of mind. Biology, particularly freshwater biology, mussels, clams—that's what mainly interests him. He has trouble being open about stuff. Like feelings, I mean."

I laughed briefly.

"What?" she said, annoyed.

"I'm not laughing at your father," I said quickly. "It's just that my parents are the opposite. My dad's very open about most everything, but my mom's way more reserved."

"Shit! This is not going anywhere!" Laura said abruptly, and stood up.

"What do you mean?" I said, surprised.

"This is just . . . talk. We're not getting anywhere." She was suddenly very agitated.

"But—"

"The bottom line is that we have to make our parents get a grip, stop this shit, so nobody else gets hurt."

"You're preaching to the choir," I said.

"Then do something!" she said, her face contorted. "Help me!" Suddenly she covered her eyes with her hands. I stared as she began to cry—ugly, shoulder-heaving, blubbering kind of crying.

"What can I do?" I said stupidly. "Tell me and I'll do it."

But she didn't hear me. She choked out, "I worry that my mom and your dad might be made for each other," she choked out. "I'm pretty sure they're in love and want to get married."

CHAPTER TEN

A true test of character is how you react when someone starts to cry.
Me, I stood up suddenly, as if I had a plan—then froze. I had
no idea of what to do. Not a freaking clue. She stood there,
in the middle of this beautiful pine grove, clutching her face
with both hands and weeping.

"Hey, look," I said, stepping closer.

Her shoulders heaved violently.

"Hey, don't, come on now," I said. I touched her shoulder—and she recoiled as if stung.

"Don't you ever touch me!" she screamed, and stared at
me wild-eyed. Then it was like she heard herself, or saw herself, and was embarrassed—which made her weep harder.
She plopped down on the ground and sat there, head in
hands, crying up a storm.

I went over and sat next to her on the ground. But not
too close.

Gradually she stopped blubbering, and her shoulders
stopped hiccuping up and down.

"You're gonna be fine, please," I said softly. Though I wanted to, I made sure not to touch her.

"I'm just so scared," she wheezed, still not looking at me.

I was silent.

"Not for me," she said. "But for my dad. And for my little sister especially. They won't be able to handle this. I think I could handle it, but I know they couldn't—especially Jenny. She's already a mess. Takes Ritalin. Sees a shrink once a week."

"Handle what?" I pressed; I could care less about her weird sister.

"A divorce, for God's sakes!" She looked up at me wild-eyed again and runny-nosed. "D-I-V-O-R-C-E. There, I've spelled it out for you. What the hell do you think we're talking about?"

"We don't know exactly what we're talking about," I countered. "You're way ahead of yourself. Nobody has said anything about a divorce. Right now we've got two adults having an affair, that's all."

"That's all," she said sarcastically.

"Hey, in the history of the human race, it's not as if this has never happened before," I said, trying for the old Jed Berg tone.

She wiped her eyes with her fists, then leaned to the side and, using her thumb, honked both channels of her nose onto the grass. I was impressed.

I continued. "And when *we* do talk to them, there's a good

chance they'll get a grip and they'll stop and this will all go away."

She shrugged. Then she looked at me, as if noticing for the first time that I was sitting on the ground beside her.

"Sorry to lose it there," she said. She stood up quickly and clapped some pine needles from her hands.

"No big deal," I said. I remained on the ground; I began to flip a pinecone hand to hand. It felt like a successful gesture, me remaining sitting on the ground, her standing.

She checked her wristwatch. "Maybe we've had enough for one day."

"Yeah. Probably. But answer me one thing," I said.

"What?"

"You've got the photos, you've got this airtight case—so why haven't you talked to your mom yet?"

"Because I'm a selfish, bad person."

I looked up at her, puzzled.

"Actually, I wanted you to do the dirty work," she said. "Get your father to break it off, and then it would be over. My mother would never know that I knew."

"And you could keep your perfect life at Ely High," I finished.

She was silent.

"Your friends. Your kayaking. Your cool, problem-free existence as Laura Sanborn, All-American."

"It would help if you were dumb," she said.

"Say what?" I had never met a girl who could make me angrier faster.

"When I finally met you—and I knew I would someday, I guess—I hoped you'd be this dumb jerk of a person. That way I could hate you and your family even more."

"Well, sorry to disappoint you—again!"

She let out a small snort of laugh, then reached down to me. I glared at her, then took her hand. She hoisted me to my feet with a hard yank upward. We let go of each other's hands immediately.

"Now what?" she said. Her blue eyes were suddenly scared.

"We talk to them," I said. "Tonight."

At home, dinner was agonizing. I wondered how it was going at the Sanborn house.

"You off your feed, Jed?" my father said. He noticed me toying with my pork chop.

"A little bit," I mumbled.

"I've noticed that you've haven't been very hungry lately," my mother added.

"Got a lot on my mind," I said. I couldn't look up at them.

"Anything we can help with?" my mother said.

"Nah, I'll take care of it," I said.

My father was silent.

After supper, the gods were with me. Or against me. Sometimes it's hard to tell. Anyway, it was a warm spring evening, and so my mother went walking with a neighbor woman—which left me alone in the kitchen with my father. We did the dishes in silence.

"So what is it, son?" my father said at length. "Girl problems? Cassie?" He smiled.

"No," I said. I took a breath. *Say, Dad?* "It's Mrs. Sanborn. From Ely."

There was a long moment of nothingness in the room—like time, our lives, the whole universe—stood still.

Then tilted.

My father let out a long breath. "Oh Jeddy," he said. He turned to me and sagged against the kitchen counter.

"I'm sorry!" I said quickly. Which was a stupid thing to say. Then, even stupider, my face scrunched itself around my eyes, which suddenly began to burn and threatened to spill over. I covered them with my hands.

"I was going to tell you" was all he could say. Over and over. I kept my face covered to hide my shame—or maybe his—and I never saw him cross the room. Suddenly he was holding me tight, like I was two years old. We just stood there, arms around each other, hanging on like we were leaning into a cold wind.

CHAPTER ELEVEN

Family life is like the stock market. There are ups and downs, peaks and valleys; but that night was the Berg family's Great Crash. After the scene with my father—we really didn't talk much more than I described—I went to my room and stayed there. I kept the door wide open and pretended to do homework. Indifference—that was the best way to punish him, I figured. I was more angry at myself for blubbering than I was at him for being a cheat.

Once he came up the stairs and looked in. He was ashen. He looked ten years older.

"What?" I said angrily, and turned back to my computer.

"Have you spoken with your mother?"

"No," I said. "Have you?"

I kept typing as if I were very busy. When I looked up again, he was gone. On my screen was:

Tjhe quick bronw fox jumps ober the lazy dog
The guick bronw fox jumps over the laxy gofg
The quick bronw fox jumps voer the lazy bog

I kept typing it over and over, faster and faster. Jack Nicholson, the crazy writer in *The Shining*—that was me.

Once I got up and peeked downstairs. My father was just sitting there on the couch, white-faced, waiting for my mother. I retreated to my room.

Not much later I heard my mother come back. The front door clicked and latched. She said something cheerful, then added, "Garrett—what's wrong?" It was if she thought he was having a heart attack.

"There's something we have to talk about," my father said.

I closed my door and turned up an old Rage Against the Machine CD. Later I took a chance and turned down the volume; actually, I thought I'd heard a noise. Weirdly, it was the vacuum cleaner. Its whirring noise moved back and forth. I gathered up courage and looked downstairs. My mother, with her jaw set like iron and her face white as bone, was vacuuming. First lengthwise, then crossways. She just kept vacuuming the living room. I ducked back into my room.

Suddenly the vacuum cleaner shut off, and its sound was replaced by my mother screaming at my father: totally lost-it shrieking rage.

"Please," he kept saying, "listen to me. Get a grip. Please."

"Get out! Just get out!" I was glad we were not a family that hunted, that had guns in the house. The front door slammed so hard, something fell from the wall and crashed to the floor, and then I heard the sharp squeal of tire rubber.

In the bathroom, I threw up, long heaving spews that splashed in the toilet bowl and spattered back on my face. The puke finally stopped coming, and then I washed up and brushed my teeth. When I crossed the hall back to my room, the vacuum cleaner was whirring again.

At my computer I looked for news from Laura. I had e-mailed her 8:12 P.M.; it was 11:10 and I'd heard nothing. Now that I had barfed, my mind felt clearer, and a dark thought grew: I'd been double-crossed. She had, after all, gotten me to do the dirty work. She was not going to speak with her mother.

A slow, black rage began to build. I began to imagine beating her up—if I actually could—wrestling her to the ground, punching her right in her wide, perfect mouth. Then I got mail.

Jed--
I did it. Showed her the photos, told her everything. She cried, then made me take Jenny downtown for a while so she could tell my dad. But Jenny's no fool. She knew something bad was happening. When we got back, an hour later, my father stood at the window, his neck blotchy. My mother was crying. My father didn't even see us. I took Jenny to my room. About a half hour ago my father went crazy. He went to the kitchen and smashed all the

dishes. One by one. Real hard onto the floor. Every time one broke, Jenny let out a shriek. The police came and my dad tried to wrestle or fight them or something, and they took him away.

I can't believe this is happening. It's like everything in my life is suddenly broken.

Laura

P.S. So what's the good news from Duluth?

I stared at the screen. I felt like there was this knob of wood or metal in my throat. I couldn't even swallow.

Laura,

Call me (555-4389) if you need to.

I didn't think it would be that bad at your house. You said your father was the logical one.

I'm so sorry. . . .

I told my father tonight too.

Then he told my mother. She went nuts at first--then got this quiet weirdness about her, and started to clean the house. She's still doing it. I don't know where my father is. I don't know what's going on. Maybe I should call my sisters. Anyway, like I said, it went fine (ha). They say humor keeps us from going crazy.

Jed

I sat there listening to the vacuum cleaner.

Hey Jed,

I think staying in our normal (ha!) routines might keep us from going crazy. Jenny's in my bed crying and sucking her thumb (eleven years old!), but I guess I can cut her some slack tonight. I even told her she could sleep with me. And why not call your sisters? You shouldn't have to hang there by yourself--not to be confused with hanging yourself--ha ha. Sorry, black humor.

L.

P.S. Maybe you could send your mother to our house to clean up all the smashed stuff.

P.P.S. I need to sign off for tonight.

She didn't call, which probably meant she was okay. I tried to sleep as best I could but woke up every half hour or so. *Was it real or was it a dream?* I kept getting lost somewhere in the middle. In the morning, when I stumbled downstairs at my regular time, I was not certain.

But there were only two places set for breakfast.

"Good morning, Jed," my mother said. She manufactured a smile that never made it to her eyes, both of which looked terrible.

I pretended not to notice anything different.

"Sorry about last night," she said; her gaze was jumpy and crazy. "Your father told me about your talk. We had ours, and then I kind of lost it."

"I heard," I said.

She began to wipe down the sink, going back over the same spot with the sponge as if the motion helped her think. "I asked him to leave," she said. "It's fairly normal in these situations. Some time apart gives everybody a chance to calm down and think things through. He's at the Super 8 Motel on Highway 61. You can reach him there if you like."

I shrugged and rattled my Rice Krispies into a bowl. As I poured milk, the snap, crackle, and pop was deafening.

"So what are you feeling right now?" she asked.

"Hungry?" I said.

"Please, Jed," she began. Her eyes were beginning to redden fast, and she came up behind me and touched my shoulder. I flinched.

She burst into tears and covered her face. I felt shitty about that but didn't do anything except continue eating. She occupied herself with dishes. I ate in silence. Then she said, "Would you like to talk to someone about this, Jed?"

"What, like a shrink?"

"More like a counselor," she said. "I know some good ones through my work."

"The thing of it is I'm not the one who's gone crazy around here."

She fell silent, then begin to weep softly again. I kept eating.

"Gotta go," I said finally, in my cheerful voice. I bussed my bowl to the immaculate sink. "School, you know."

* * *

I went to my first-period class. I sat in the same desk as always. Everything was in order except that my teacher spoke a strange language. Arabic? Chinese? Klingon? I mean, I've taken Spanish, and once went to a summer camp for French, and my sister Melanie used to practice her German on me, but this was weird.

After class Bobby came up to me. "Juan downers hokay?"

"Say what?" I said.

"I said, 'You on downers today?'" he replied loudly. "Geez, what's the matter with you?"

I thought about that for a long moment. "My dad moved out last night," I said. Even I heard the strange tone in my voice; I felt totally calm, a blankness in my face, like I'd had an overdose of novocaine.

"Oh, is that all?" Bobby said.

I blinked. I looked at him closely for the first time. His acne was really flaring up—red welts strung along his cheeks and neck like blackfly bites. I thought of canoeing with my father; I wondered if we'd ever do that again.

"It's a freaking joke, Jed," Bobby said. But one little blank spot in his eyes was clearly thinking about his own "family"; about how that might play out.

I put a hand on his shoulder and leaned closer. I felt like hitting him, hard.

"Get a grip, Jed," Bobby said. "Cassie is coming our way."

I let go of Bobby.

"Hey, Jed, when are you going to drive the Chevy again?" Cassie said coyly. She touched my arm.

I stared at her. She actually had a pimple. A small one, like a mosquito bite, on her left cheek, but a pimple nonetheless. "The Chevy? Probably never," I said. My words came out in the same calm, blank tone; I couldn't see myself asking my father for the Chevy ever again. I couldn't see myself asking him for anything. I kept staring at Cassie. "By the way, you have a pimple." I didn't mean anything by it; I just felt the need to be completely honest for once.

Her hand shot up to her face; she blushed angrily. "What is *wrong* with him?" she said to Bobby as she turned away.

"Oh, nothing," Bobby called after her. "His parents just split up."

At my locker, I stared down for the longest time at my combination lock. I couldn't think of any of the numbers. Not one. And I had to put away my books. All I wanted to do was put away my books. The lock pissed me off. I began to kick at the lock, then punch my locker; I kicked it again and again and began to swear at it. Nearby, girls shrieked and scattered. The locker caved in gradually, and—just when the door gave way enough for me to slide in my books—strong arms grabbed me from behind. It was a security guard, Boyd, backed up by

Vice-Principal Hartness and my English teacher, Mr. Stinson. Together they hustled me, shouting and swearing, off to the office. "My lock doesn't work, you bastards—my lock doesn't work!" I kept shouting.

In the vice-principal's office, it was like I woke up. I was sitting in a straight-backed wooden chair with three adult males staring down at me.

"What do you think you're doing!" the security guard began. He was a burly, younger guy with a shaved head.

"Just a minute, Boyd," Mr. Stinson interrupted. "I'll handle this."

The security guard glowered. "Nobody swears at me. That's a three-day, for sure!"

"Please, Boyd," Mr. Stinson said.

The vice-principal nodded; Mr. Stinson began the interrogation. "What happened, Jed?"

"What happened?" I repeated. I tried to sound like myself. The smooth, unflappable, well-liked Jed Berg. "Well, I've had so much trouble with my lock, and with that door in general—I mean, every day it takes me several extra minutes to just get my books," I said, lying through my teeth. "The stress just built up, I guess. I had a little bit of a bad day, too, and I guess the frustration, as they say, boiled over." I smiled weakly.

"No kidding," the security guard growled.

"I really apologize for losing my grip. It was totally out of character for me," I continued. "And certainly I'll pay for the locker." I was finding my groove, my smooth talk.

The adults looked at one another.

"Jed is a fine student, never been a problem in my classes," Mr. Stinson said. "I tend to agree—it was very out of character."

"So? He still trashed the locker in front of the whole school and swore at me," Boyd growled.

The vice-principal hoisted one hoary eyebrow. "Boyd, you're correct. But Mr. Stinson is onto something here, too. That did seem very out of character for you, Jed. We could suspend you for three full days; however, I'm recommending detention after school for the rest of the week, as well as a talk with one of our counselors about anger management."

"Thank you, sir," I said. "Anger management. I think that's very wise, indeed, sir."

They all looked me—the security guard pissed, the vice-principal pleased, Mr. Stinson still a bit puzzled.

"Detention begins right after last period," Boyd said, "and goes until four thirty P.M."

"I have tennis practice after school," I said.

He grinned for the first time. "No you don't."

CHAPTER TWELVE

I always thought detention was for other people. But here I was, in the library with the other after-school losers, about ten of them slumped along reading tables like roadkill on the shoulders of a highway to hell. Most already had their heads on their arms, and cap bills pulled low over their eyes. I signed in at the detention monitor's desk.

"Name?" said Mr. Thompson, one of the shop teachers. I thought everybody knew my name.

"Jed Berg," I answered. Cheerfully. As if this were a mistake. As if Mr. Thompson would immediately understand the error.

"Hey! Berg!" someone said; Derek Jones lifted his head from his arms.

I glanced at him.

"You lost, or what?"

A couple of other rough-looking dudes lifted their heads from their arms and squinted sleepily at me. "He's slummin'," one of them said.

"Quiet in here—you know the rules," Thompson barked at the losers. "Take a seat, Berg," he ordered with a jerk of his head.

A skinny, black-eyeliner chick glared at me as I passed; I had seen her around. She reminded me of weird Jenny, Laura's little sister.

"Seriously, what are you doing in here, man?" Derek whispered.

"Little problem with my locker door," I muttered, taking a chair a two seats away. I certainly wasn't going to sit by him.

"Hey—you the dude that caved his locker in right in front of Boyd?" one of the losers said, perking up.

"That's me." I settled in near the bookshelves.

"Cool, man!" another said. "We heard about that. All right, dude!" The motor heads and other losers looked at me with sudden respect. *My new fan club. Great.*

"Maybe there's hope for you after all," Derek said.

"Quiet!" Thompson thundered.

I ignored them all and got out my homework. At least I could make use of my time. I glanced toward the entrance; the doors were open to the main hallway. Maybe people passing would think I was working on a history paper or something.

As the losers settled their heads down to sleep, the skinny chick kept staring at me. I tried to read, but she stared unblinkingly.

"What the hell are you looking at?" I finally said.

"You," she said.

"Why don't you look out the freaking window or something?"

"I like looking at you," she said. "Preppies in a downward spiral are fun to watch." On her arms I noticed a fine mesh of little cut marks, like tribal scars, plus a couple of seriously red and festery spots.

"Cigarette burns," she said. "Want to know who did them?"

"Not really," I said. I looked down at my homework and tried to concentrate on my algebra. I tried for several minutes, but the numbers looked backward or upside down. I switched to English and tried to read some Faulkner but kept getting lost in the sentences; I'd forget where they began and have to keep going back and starting over. I glanced around. Jenkins was busy with his grade book. Derek and the losers were all dozing; the skinny chick was drawing flower petals, in red ink, around one of her cigarette burns. She was a good artist; the bright flower petals unfolding on her arm could attract bees.

I turned to the bookshelf that was within arm's reach. It was the geography section: oversize map-type books. One caught my eye: *Canada: Great Neighbor to the North*. I reached over and pulled it off the shelf. For some reason I had always worried about ending up on *Wheel of Fortune* or *Jeopardy!* and losing big money because I didn't know something really simple, such as the Canadian provinces.

"Berg—put back the book!" Mr. Thompson growled.

All the losers jerked awake and looked groggily around.

"Excuse me?" I said. I had already opened the big book to the map plates.

His lips moved again but his words made no sense.

I stared at him. "What?" I just kept looking at him.

He stood up. "You got wax buildup in your ears, Berg?"

"No," I said.

"*Parlez-vous* English?"

"Yes," I said.

Around me, all the losers were fully awake now.

"What I said was 'Put back the book.' This is detention," Mr. Thompson said. "You can't read library books during detention."

I looked down at the book. I looked around at the shelves of books. "Why not?" I asked.

"Because I say so."

I looked around. The others were grinning at me; even the skinny chick had stopped drawing on her arm.

"But this is a library," I said.

"No, it's detention."

The whole scene was like a movie with frames missing

and bits of dialogue cut out. Everything was choppy and jerky, and Thompson was suddenly moving toward me. In an instant he towered over me. I could smell oil and metal lathes and motors on his clothes; his fingers were thick and his fingernails framed by little horseshoes of black grease.

"Berg, either put back the frigging book or you get detention all next week with this great little group of ours."

I looked around. The other students stared back at me. For a long moment I saw them as just kids, as if they were in grade school and everything was fine and their lives hadn't yet gone into the toilet.

"I just want to review the Canadian provinces," I said. "That's all." I was completely serious. *One should know the Canadian provinces.*

"Okay, have it your way, Berg," Mr. Thompson said. He yanked the book from my hands.

"I was putting it back!" I said.

"I didn't see it," he said.

"They saw it," I said, turning to the others, "didn't you?"

They stared at me in silence; the skinny chick, her eyes suddenly human for the first time, looked down at her pink-and-red skin flower.

"I don't think they saw it," Mr. Thompson said. He slammed the book back into its slot. "And neither did I. Which means I'll see you here all next week, too, Mr. Berg."

I looked up at him. My eyes started to fill and burn, and he began to swim back to the front of the room. In my only successful gesture of day, I lurched up from my seat and gave him the one-finger salute—which brought a great laugh from all my new friends.

Luckily tennis practice ran until five thirty P.M., which meant I could make the last half of it.

"Where the hell have you been?" Mr. Burns asked as I trotted up with my bag. He was a younger teacher, very fit, very serious, with a deadly left-hand stroke. His real life should have been professional tennis, but something made his personal wheel of fortune slip a cog; now he was a high school civics teacher and tennis coach.

"Sorry," I said. Seeing all the tennis kids in their whites, whacking the yellow-green balls back and forth, grunting and laughing and calling to each other—it made me feel like I was back. Back in my real life.

"I had an appointment," I explained, hurriedly unzipping my bag. It was enough of an excuse to get by; after all, I was number-one singles.

"Well, get loose. You been missing way too much practice lately."

"Sorry, coach."

I stretched and then joined Bobby for some volleys.

"'Appointment'?" Bobby whispered. "Coach is not gonna like that when he finds out you got detention."

"*If* he finds out," I replied, "I'll figure out something." I slammed a forehand past him. Except that it didn't get past him; Bobby dropped a knee and looped a backhand over my head. I couldn't catch up to it.

"Hey—what are you doing? I'm not loose," I called angrily.

He grinned and backed off as we volleyed. Slowly I could feel my legs loosening out, my stroke returning.

"You see the challenge board?" Bobby asked.

"No."

"Soren Smith thinks he's ready for you."

I glanced over. Soren, a skinny left-handed sophomore, looked at me, then quickly away. I glared at him.

"Is that right, Smith? You challenge me?"

"Ah, yes?"

"Fine. Bring it on," I called. The anger in my voice surprised me.

"When?" he answered, stroking a ball past his partner.

"Anytime," I answered, chipping one in front of Bobby, making him lunge.

"I'd thought about today," Soren said apologetically. "Unless you want to wait."

The tone of his voice pissed me off. He said it like there

might be extenuating circumstances, like I might have had enough for one day; but what really pissed me off more was that he was trying to be nice.

"Why would I need to wait?" I replied. I looked around; everybody was staring. It suddenly hit me that everybody knew about my old man. I turned to Bobby.

"Thanks a lot," I muttered.

"Hey, I only told Cassie. And a couple of girls in our grade."

"Why didn't you just put it on the radio?" I said.

I went at him with hard smashes, and he did his best to keep up. When I was good and sweaty, I motioned Bobby off the court. "Let's go, Smith," I called.

Forty-five minutes later, at 4–6, 6–5, 1–6, I was number-two singles. "Game," I said to Soren; we shook hands at the net.

"Thanks!" he said, leaning back slightly as if I might hit him with my racket. I turned away.

"I can't believe it!" Smith called out like a kid. "I beat Jed Berg!"

Some of his sophomore pals clapped and laughed with him.

I walked off, my lungs burning, my legs trembling. "Tough calls," Bobby said, hurrying up to me with a towel. He lowered his voice. "It was like Coach Thom had it in for you. All those balls on the paint, Jesus!"

"Forget it—I sucked," I wheezed.

Mr. Burns came over. "So, Berg, what happened to you today?"

"My backhand," I began.

"No, with detention," he said. "Your 'appointment.'"

I stared. Suddenly Bobby and everybody nearby got very busy putting away their gear.

"It's a long story," I said.

He shrugged, checked his watch. "I've got time."

Around me, my tennis pals oozed away like water through gutter grates; suddenly Coach Burns and I were pretty much alone.

Hey, you asked for it. I looked straight at him. "My parents split up yesterday." He blinked. Tilted back almost imperceptibly on his rubber soles. He was silent; I began to put away my stuff.

"Actually, your backhand did suck," the coach said.

I looked up.

"You weren't turning over your leading wrist," he added. "Want to see what I mean?"

I nodded. He grabbed a racket and we put the net between us.

We volleyed a couple of times; then he began to work with me. "Stretch it out, elongate your arm," he called.

I obeyed.

"To get a stroke back, to recover a motion—any kind of athletic motion—you need to exaggerate it," he said. He showed me, in slow motion, rolling his forearm until his elbow was fully sideways.

I followed suit.

"That's it," he said.

We continued. I started to stroke some balls.

"Now you're getting it back. . . .

"Follow through! Always follow through!

"That's it. . . ."

We volleyed for twenty minutes, until I was suddenly weak with hunger.

"Enough?" he called.

I nodded. Sweating, we both put away our gear.

"Thanks, coach, " I said as I turned to go.

"No problem." He paused. "By the way. Good luck with your family . . . thing."

"Thanks," I muttered. And headed home for supper.

At the big house my mother was waiting with a full steak-potatoes-and-green-salad dinner. She hadn't cooked so much in years—and for only two people.

"So, Jeddy, how was your day?" She tried to use her normal voice. Her eyes were red and puffy.

I stared at her. It occurred to me that since getting up I

had (probably) lost my girlfriend, destroyed my locker, ended up with detention all next week, plus had gotten knocked out of number-one singles.

"Could have been better," I said.

"Me too," she said. And suddenly began to weep. I crossed the foyer and held her. It was the least I could do. But it pissed me off, and she felt frail and sharp boned and lost, and I felt something in my heart turn cold.

CHAPTER THIRTEEN

At least I had e-mail.

Hi Jed. Well, how was your day? Mine was absolutely screwed. Everybody in school stared at me like I had dog shit on my shoes. Small town, you know; everybody had heard about my dad's crack-up and the police at our house. They love that sort of stuff in small towns. Anyway, right now my dad is in a motel, which is terrible because he hates motels--he doesn't like to go anywhere. And my Mom's home carrying on and cooking and doing all the normal shit as if nothing happened-- when it's all her fault. And your father's, that is.
L

I wrote back.

Laura,
Bad day doesn't describe it. Day From Hell? Before today I used to have a girlfriend, I used to be cool with my teachers, and I

used to be #1 singles in tennis. Oh--and I almost forgot--I used to have two parents. The only positive thing about today was that I did not get testicular cancer.
J

Jed,
The last part is good news.
So now what?
L

Laura,
Beats me. Really.
J

Jed,
Me too. I feel kind of blank. Like I'm living off to the side of my life--kind of looking in on it. It's very weird. BTW, sorry about your girlfriend.
L

Laura,
ECEG. Actually I think she liked me mainly for my dad's Camaro, which he let me drive. And oh, add that to my Day From Hell list: no more Camaro.

J

Jed,

Trust me, your dad will still let you drive the Camaro. He'll feel
so shitty about what he's doing that he might give it to you. He
probably feels like he's lost you. Your girlfriend did sound TGTBT.
At least I don't have a boyfriend to complicate things.

L

Laura,

He has lost me. I'll never ask him for anything again. I don't care
if I ever see him again. To hell with him. And hey--I saw all those
guys hanging around you in your school parking lot. You must
have a boyfriend.

J

Jed,

They're just friends. That's all I've ever had, in terms of boys.
I guess I've been too involved with sports to make time
for a real boyfriend. On the other hand, I could be scared,
actually. Of having a boyfriend, I mean. Not that it matters.
Why am I telling you, for God's sakes? I really don't know what
matters right now. That's how I feel. Here's something strange:
I was driving in town today and came to a stop sign.
There were no cars coming. I thought, "Why am I stopping?
This is insane, stopping for no reason." So I sped up and
drove right through it. It felt great. Except that this guy in a
pickup saw me and honked and pointed at me. I gave him the

finger. That felt great, too.
L

Laura,
Cool. The stop sign stuff, I mean. I'll have to tell you about
detention sometime--another first for me today. And BTW,
boyfriends are overrated. We're all undependable and basically
fake. If I were a girl and knew what boys' minds were really like,
I'd never date one.
J

Jed,
Hey, you need some protein or some rest. Though I know what
you mean, kind of. Girls' minds are like fireworks continually
going off. Like everything is important and everything is
happening at once. I hate that feeling. I think that's why I like
kayaking. Just me going down the lake in a straight line. I can
look ahead and see where I'm going. I can look behind and see
where I've been. I tried to get Jenny into it (kayaking), because if
anyone has no direction, it's her. We've gone into the BWCAW
camping a couple of times, and she sort of liked it. But sometimes I think she was switched at the hospital.
Rambling here. I have to do some homework. Or sleep.
Or something.
L

Laura,

You're right. I'm gonna blow off my homework and go to sleep. That's all I feel like doing, for days--just sleeping. CU.

J

Jed,

Do some homework. It would be one small victory for today. Gnight.

L

I put my computer to sleep and sat there. My bed looked inviting, but she was right about the homework; annoyed, I set to work on my algebra. Downstairs I heard my mother on the phone, sniffling some, probably talking with one of her woman friends. I put everything out of my head and forced myself to concentrate on a page of proofs. Weirdly, the numbers fell into place like dominoes, like puzzle pieces. My life might be stupid right now, but I was not. As I worked, I kept wondering what Laura was doing at this very moment.

Once I heard the phone ring and snatched up the receiver. It was my father.

"Jeddy!" he said. "It's great to—"

"Just a sec, I'll get her," I answered.

"No, wait—"

I covered up his voice with my hand and shouted for my mother. "It's him."

"Got it," she called.

I hung up. For a few seconds I stared at the phone, then went back to my homework. I was not going to let anything throw me off. I finished my physics, then began reading Faulkner's story "Barn Burning."

Downstairs, my mother's voice was suddenly loud and vile. I'd never heard her use those words before. She slammed down the phone and began to weep.

I put on headphones so I couldn't hear anything and concentrated on Faulkner's sentences and words. For a while I had to whisper each word aloud. But gradually the story pulled me in. It was set just after the Civil War, about a kid named Sartoris Snopes, whose father was a barn burner. The Snopeses were a white-trash sharecropper family, and his father always managed to get into an argument with the landowner and then burn his barn. Some family. I could already hear Katie Sorenson's objections in English class to more reading about depressing people. . . . Oddly, I looked forward to getting up and going to school tomorrow. There at least everything would be the same.

After I finished all my homework I lay in bed, thinking about my father in his motel room. I could feel him thinking about me. I thought of calling him, but I didn't.

CHAPTER FOURTEEN

"Sorry about last night," my mother said the next morning.

"How so?" I muttered. I slumped over my Rice Krispies and did not look directly at her.

"I kind of lost it on the phone. With your father."

I shrugged.

"He also wanted to talk to you, but I didn't think it was appropriate. Over the phone, that is."

"I'll decide what's appropriate!" I shot back. Among the ceramic tiles, black granite countertops, and stainless steel refrigerator, my voice was harsh and knife sharp.

She drew back. "Sure. Okay, Jed."

I watched her from the corner of my eye as she drank her coffee. Her hands shook slightly.

"Sorry. I didn't mean to snap at you," I said.

She smiled gratefully, let out a long breath. She poured herself more coffee. "This is new territory, I guess. For all of us."

I was silent. I kept eating. From habit I rustled the newspaper. There was at least one good thing about my father being gone: I didn't have to share the sports section.

"You should know," she said softly, "that your father and I have been going to marriage counseling for some time."

I looked up. "Say what?"

She repeated herself.

I stared at her.

"I just thought you should know," she said. "It might make this all more . . . explainable."

"Explainable?" I said. "Explainable?" My voice again echoed harsh and loud.

"Please, Jed," she said. "Don't curse."

I didn't realize I had. And at whom?

"Your father and I have been . . . struggling for some time," she said. "Over the years we've lost something, I think."

"I guess!" I muttered, and clattered my empty cereal bowl into the sink. Strange how when you most want to say things, your brain gives you the least vocabulary.

"I thought we were getting it back, but I guess not." She began to sniffle and turned away. When I left for school, she was no better.

"Where's your hooded sweatshirt?" she said, trying to touch me. "It's chilly today."

"It's in my locker at school—I'll be fine!" I said.

I couldn't think of anything else to say. And I couldn't even hug her.

At school there was a cop car out front. Probably the stupid DARE officer here to brainwash the ninth graders. Down the hallway to my locker bay, there was some kind of commotion—an officer and his German shepherd dog. A K-9 unit of some kind. Law-enforcement show-and-tell day. The vice-principal and Boyd, the security guard thug, were standing near my new locker (the other one was still smashed). I'd had Bobby put my stuff in it, and now I put on my cheerful voice. "Hey, Mr. Hartness, Boyd—what's going on?"

Boyd grinned at me.

"Mr. Berg?" the police officer said, stepping forward.

"Yeah?"

"Is your locker number two twenty-three?"

"Ah, yeah."

"Would you open it up please?"

"What is this, Shawshank High?" I replied. A small crowd of juniors had gathered; I didn't want to miss an opportunity for a smart remark.

"Please. Just open it, Jed," the vice-principal said.

"Sure," I said. The dog whined and strained.

As the door opened, the dog lunged forward, clamped on my hooded sweatshirt, and began to shake it like a dead cat.

Shit. Don't tell me. I can't believe this is happening.

"Kelly! Stay!" the officer shouted, and restrained the dog.

Student voices murmured around me.

"Is this your sweatshirt?" The officer carefully held it up; the dog had left slobber marks on it.

"Yes," I said. Weirdly, I began to giggle.

Kelly, on a tight leash, chewed at the right pocket. The officer yanked him back, reached inside, felt around, and gingerly extracted a fat white joint.

Compliments of Jenny Sanborn, Ely, Minnesota.

There was a giant sucking in of breath, which is very similar to the sound of one's life going down the toilet.

"Oh shit! Berg's busted! They got Berg!" People scattered to spread the news.

I began to laugh so hard, I could hardly hear them. I kept laughing all the way to the principal's office—I would have fallen down, I was laughing so hard, but Big Boyd had me by one arm and the police officer by the other. Cassie and her friends floated past, their eyes wide and horrified, and there was no shortage of other rubberneckers, including Bobby and Soren Smith from tennis.

"'They carved no hopeful verse on his tomb-stone,'" I shouted to Bobby and the others as the gendarmes hustled me off. "That's Hawthorne, by the way. You gotta read Hawthorne—he's the man!" My voice cackled hysterically in the hallway. Then I was secured inside the vice-principal's office.

There was silence.

"Well, Jed," the vice-principal said.

"A deep subject," I said, and began to laugh all the harder.

The authorities glanced sideways at each other and waited; slowly I got a grip.

"You'll want to call a parent," the vice-principal began.

The police officer nodded. "An adult, parent, or guardian will need to come and accompany you downtown."

"Downtown?" I started to giggle again.

"You think this is funny?" the officer said; he held up the joint. "You're busted, kid, and you think it's funny?"

"What is this, like the movies? I get to make one phone call?"

"Much like that," the officer replied. "Call a parent, call your attorney, it's up to you."

"How about both?" I said. "Two calls for the price of one."

"Don't get smart," Boyd growled. "What did he just say? One call."

"I can't make one call without the other," I said.

"You high or something?" Boyd said.

"No. His mother is an attorney—that's what he means," Vice-Principal Hartness said suddenly.

I dialed her cell phone. She was on her way to work. The enforcers watched and listened as I talked. "Say, Mom? There's been a . . . mix-up here at school. I need you to

come. Meet me at the vice-principal's office. Now. Please?"
I hung up. What more was there to say?

"A mix-up?" Boyd said. "That would be understatement of the day. So where'd you get the pot, anyway?"

"That would be my area," the officer said evenly to Boyd. "I'll handle that part."

"Yes, there are procedures to be observed," the vice-principal said. He was suddenly chewing on the side of his lower lip; I realized he was paranoid about my mom being a lawyer.

"Procedures like due process? Unreasonable search and seizure? Small things like that?" I said to the officer.

His lips narrowed. He, too, was suddenly all professional.

As I waited for my mom, I clammed up. My silence seemed to rattle the vice-principal.

"Procedures were followed, there's no doubt about that, yes?" he said to the officer. "Lots of witnesses. Subject was asked to open his locker and complied. Voluntarily. Of course no search-and-seizure problems there, right?"

The officer nodded.

The vice-principal began to page through a three-ring binder and mutter to himself. "Yes, here we are. Everything seems to be according to Hoyle."

"That would be Edmond Hoyle, English authority on card games," I said, "but not an attorney, I think." I felt more

133

laughter coming on, waves of it, the same muscle used for throwing up.

"If you're so smart, how come you ended up with dope in your locker?" the officer asked. He was a professional non-smiler.

"Who says it's mine? Who says it's even dope?" I said.

A fine line of sweat began to form just above the vice-principal's top lip.

"We'll see about that after your attorney comes," the officer said. "But if Kelly says it's dope, it's probably dope—right Kelly?"

We all looked at Kelly. He wagged his tail wildly. Kelly's real life should have been chasing rabbits in the country; instead, he had to ride around in the backseat of a patrol car, inhaling auto exhaust and listening to the squawk of police radios.

And then, thankfully, my mother entered. I felt like weeping; I felt like I was six years old.

"What's going on here?" she asked immediately. She's not a tall woman but has eyes and clothes that mean business. That and a killer black briefcase.

The vice-principal cleared his throat. "Mrs. Berg, I'm sorry to say that Jed has—at least so it appears—been found to have marijuana in his locker."

She laughed. It was great, actually, to hear it. At first one involuntary chuckle, then a full-bodied, from-the-gut laugh. I hadn't heard that from her in years. "I'm guessing there's some kind of mistake here," she said soon enough, looking to me. "Yes, Jed?"

"For sure," I said.

"So let's get this cleared up," she said, turning to the officer. "I have work to do. We all have work to do."

"'Fraid it's not that simple, ma'am," the officer began. As he spoke, I could see, through my mother's eyes, her brain working, her thoughts whirring and clicking; of course she knew this wasn't simple, but it had been worth a try. Sweet.

"Then as his mother—and his counsel—I must ask you to please tell me everything that has happened so far." She whipped out a yellow legal pad and a pen.

The officer looked toward the VP. He cleared his throat again and began. "As you know, under the State of Minnesota legal code, this being a public, that is to say taxpayer-supported, institution—"

"Of course," my mother said impatiently.

"We have the right, therefore, to unannounced, periodic, and random locker checks for illegal materials."

"Weapons and drugs. That's what we check for," Boyd said.

"It so happened that Kelly—" the policeman began.

"And who's Kelly?" my mother interrupted.

"Our police dog. A German shepherd trained at the police

academy in Minneapolis."

"All right," she said, glancing down at the dog.

"Kelly, here, smelled something suspicious in locker number two twenty-three," the vice-principal said.

My mother turned to me; I shrugged.

"Are you sharing a locker with anyone, Jed? No, don't answer that." She turned back to the adults. "So when did this search happen? Who was there? Who witnessed it?"

"It happened just before school this morning; several of us were there—including many students," the vice-principal said.

She was silent.

"In short, I think the school is well within its rights here, Mrs. Berg," he added.

"Under the circumstances, Jed will have to appear before the school judicial conduct board because of the controlled substance—"

"Alleged controlled substance," my mother interjected.

"'Alleged controlled substance,' yes," the officer said. "It will be analyzed for content, and, assuming it is cannabis, then Jed will become a part of the criminal court system." He turned to me. "How old are you?"

I was mum.

"Sixteen, which means juvenile court," my mother said.

"Probably. But not always," the officer replied. "That

will be determined later."

"And in terms of school policies?" my mother asked.

The vice-principal cleared his throat. "As I believe you know, Jed is currently in after-school detention for destruction of school property."

My mother turned to look at me.

"I'd been meaning to tell you," I said.

"He destroyed his locker," Boyd said helpfully.

My mother bit her lip, then turned back to the principal.

"The locker incident, along with some insubordination during detention, and now a controlled-substance violation—"

"Alleged controlled substance," my mother said automatically.

"Assuming the worst, Jed can be suspended for three weeks, with possible expulsion for the remainder of the school year."

I blinked. It was amazing how small bad things added up.

"How is this possible?" my mother asked in a stunned, mother's voice this time.

"Violation and punishment policies are in the student handbook mailed to every home at the beginning the school year," the vice-principal said, gaining confidence. "It's all in the section called 'Student Misconduct.'"

Who reads that stuff? I always thought it was for other people.

"Hey—what about my detention?" I said suddenly. "If I'm suspended, how am I supposed to serve detention?" I began to giggle.

All four adults looked at me.

"Sorry," I muttered. And laughed once. But it did not sound like me laughing.

"By 'assuming the worst' you mean that the alleged controlled substance is actually that," my mother added.

"Of course. Most certainly," the vice-principal said.

It occurred to me that one of the main roles of lawyers in society was to force people to be more polite. That, and to remember people's exact words several sentences prior.

Everybody was silent.

"So now what?" I asked.

"I'd like you to take Jed home for today," the vice-principal said. "I don't want any further disruption in the hallways."

"Don't I have to, like, 'go downtown'?" I asked. I looked at the officer; I could feel the giggles coming on again.

"If you don't shut up, that could very well happen," my mother whispered from the side of her mouth.

Luckily, as I left, classes had started, so the hallways were empty except for a few tardy losers. Not to be confused with me, Jed Berg, being escorted out the door by a police officer and my mother. One of my cap-boy detention pals gave me an admiring, double-longhorn salute.

In the Lexus my mother was silent. Steely, knife-edged, hair-trigger silent. She slowly put the car in gear.

"There's always Mexico," I began.

"Don't," she said ominously.

I shrugged, and slouched lower in the seat.

We rode along for a full block. "You know, Jed," she said, turning to me, "I really didn't need this. Not right now, for God's sakes."

I looked at her. All I could do was laugh.

"What is the matter with you?" she asked. She pulled abruptly to a stop. "What the hell is the *matter* with you!" Suddenly she was shouting.

I waited until my mother got a grip—literally—on the steering wheel.

"Maybe he should take me home?" I said, nodding to the patrol car ahead.

It's amazing how mean we can be; how there's no bottom to our human capacities for cruelty.

Actually, we didn't drive straight home. My mother turned back toward the school.

I looked at her questioningly.

"You'll need your books," she said.

"True," I said. One-word responses seemed best right now.

We parked out front. "Wait here," she said. She took the keys with her and pointed her remote at the car. *Kachunk-*

kachunk went the locks. *Thanks for the symbolic vote of confidence, Ma.*

I sat in the Lexus and stared at the school. At its old, wide brick face. The pale, decorative granite above the main entrance; the brick arches above the windows; the cornices and the high, flat roofline. There were lots of neat little architectural things I'd never noticed.

I looked down at my mother's little dashboard calendar. Three weeks.

That would bring me to the end of school. Tennis season (forget that) would be winding down. Senior prom would have come and gone; I had had a vision of going in the Camaro with Cassie. But hey, ECEG. I made a mental list of all the other things I would miss, but there were so many, I kept forgetting where I'd begun.

I must have dozed briefly; I wasn't really sleeping, but suddenly the locks chirped and my mother was settling into the driver's seat. She carried a large bag of books, and her face was grim.

"What took so long?" I said.

"I wanted to speak with all your teachers. Get your books. Make arrangements for homework," she said.

Three weeks' worth of assignments. I was exhausted just thinking about it.

"But they'd *prefer not to do that*," she said angrily.

I turned quickly toward her. "What do you mean?"

"I mean that for any suspension longer than two weeks, the student and his family must make *alternative educational plans*."

"Like what?"

She looked at me. "They went through the various options, including a tutor, homeschooling, or an alternative school."

I laughed. "You don't mean, like, Oakleaf?"

She stared at me, then started the engine and began to drive. "We don't know. We're going to have to make a plan. A family plan," she added sarcastically.

I watched the school parking lot recede behind me. I knew those cars, those trucks—nearly every one.

"Right now I have a judge who is angry at me," my mother said. "So I'm going to take you home, where you'll stay the rest of the day, and I will return to work. The first thing you'll do when you get home is take some responsibility for your actions and call your father. You and he can talk this over. Come up with some ideas. When I get home, you can let me know what you've discussed. I'd prefer not to see him in person right now—I'm sure you understand—but somehow we'll get this done. We'll talk about the marijuana thing later."

Hey, Mom, want to know where I got the dope?

"Is that okay with you?" Her eyes bored into mine.

Hey, Mom, want to know why this all happened?

"Sure," I said.

At home, the house was large and silent. It was 10:32 A.M. I should be in advanced algebra right now. I tossed the heavy book bag on the couch. I flipped on the television and sat there. Reruns of Bob Barker on *The Price Is Right* came on. I turned down the sound; I couldn't bear to hear the idiots shrieking and sucking up to Bob, so I watched their mouths move, the wheels spin, the arrows point.

The price of things. I watched people take their best guess. People in the audience soundlessly screamed their advice.

"Lower!" I said to a saggy woman; a bedroom set—mattress and box spring and headboard, plus two dressers—could not cost four thousand dollars, no way.

But it was higher: retail, $5,995. "Hey, don't listen to me," I said. I didn't know the cost of anything. And suddenly she had a new bedroom set. She hugged Bob Barker so hard, I thought she would break his skinny old neck.

I clicked off the TV. I felt short of breath. I was either having a heart attack or a life-defining moment.

Or both.

I got up and went to the refrigerator. "I'm sorry," I said to it. I had no idea what I meant, but it seemed appropriate. Automatically I got out the stuff for a sandwich: bread, turkey, lettuce, mayo. I took my time putting it all together and then carefully cut it diagonally. Two perfect right triangles. I arranged some Doritos in the middle, and two Gedney dill pickle halves on the sides. I wanted it to be just right.

I poured a glass of milk.

Found a paper napkin, folded it into a tidy triangle.

Then I sat down to eat. I made myself go slowly. I realized I never thought much about eating; I always just plopped down and wolfed my food. Now I made myself sit straight and chew each bite several times. After a few minutes of this, I felt myself begin to relax.

When I finished lunch, I put things away and tidied up so that there was no sign of human presence, just the way my mother liked it.

After that I went to the phone. The Super 8 Motel number was scrawled on a piece of paper. I picked up the receiver, then put it down.

In my room I powered up my Mac and checked my e-mail. No mail, and Laura was not on-line. Then again, most seventeen-year-olds tended to be in school about right now.

I went back downstairs. Picked up the phone again. I dialed the number, then suddenly hung up. For some reason I went to his study; lots of his stuff, including his blueprints, T-square, and drawing pencils, was gone. I looked out the window to the street.

A few minutes later I was driving the Camaro—carefully—downhill, headed for the Super 8 Motel. I drove like a little old lady: The last thing I needed right now was an accident. But soon enough I was there. I saw the Ford Explorer and felt a surge of hope; he was home. So to speak. And my father was not like my mother; he didn't go crazy when small things—or even big things—happened. I would tell him everything, and he would listen and nod and squint his eyes as he considered things. "Hey, we need a plan," he would say. Either that or "Looks like we got to get organized."

Get organized. That's what I needed to do.

I stopped at the main desk.

"Berg?" the clerk said. She was a youngish, overweight woman with dull eyes. "He's in twenty A."

I trotted up the stairs, hurrying now, in a rush to see him just like I used to be when I came home from grade school. Twenty A. I rapped quickly on the door. "Dad?" I called. "It's me."

There were sounds. A woman's voice—and sudden rustling scrambling noises. I listened. Urgent whispering. I stepped and checked the door's number: 20A. For some reason I looked behind me, down and over the balcony. There, parked not far from me, was the Sanborns' black Jeep Cherokee.

Don't tell me.

I pulled back my hand. Unclenched my fist. In slow motion, I turned to leave, and made it all the way into the parking lot before my father appeared on the balcony.

"Jed!" he called. "Wait!"

I turned. He was fully dressed but his hair was mussed and wild. Plus his shirt was buttoned wrong and not tucked all the way in. I stared up at him. At my father, the stranger.

CHAPTER FIFTEEN

Leaving the parking lot, I braked at Highway 61; there was a gap in traffic but I sat there, hand poised over the skinny turn-signal arm. There was a small matter of direction. As in which way to turn. Not to mention what to do, who to talk to—little things like that.

In my rearview mirror I saw my father trotting across the parking lot toward me, tucking in his shirt, waving for me to come back.

I squealed the tires as I turned north, toward Ely. Why not? Laura's mother was out of town (clearly), my mother was out to lunch with rage, both fathers were in their motels—so why not go see Laura?

Heading out of town in the Camaro, I forced myself to watch the speed limit. Last thing I needed today was a ticket.

Fifty minutes later I passed by The White Pines, where Laura and I had talked honestly for the first time. I had a surge of emotion; felt my eyes burn at the memory of meeting her there. I shook my head to clear it; maybe I was cracking up. I concentrated on driving as the straight road eventually went narrow and winding. I concentrated on just getting to Ely in one piece.

I braked hard at the city limits sign—was going almost seventy—and soon turned left on Sheridan toward the school. I cruised the parking lot and saw her blue car, then parked in a handicapped spot and bounded up the steps. For some odd reason I remembered her schedule from Derek's computer hacking. My luck continued: Classes had just changed, and the students in the hallway were filtering toward classroom doors, some of which were closing.

"Hey, could you tell me where senior English is?" I asked.

Two girls looked at me strangely, then pointed. "Take a left; it's halfway down on the right."

I pressed on. A few students were milling near the door, laughing with the woman teacher; I slipped behind them into the room.

"Laura!" a girl said urgently. "It's that guy! That same guy!"

Laura, of course already at her desk, looked up. She was tired around the edges of her eyes; she looked older, changed, twenty-one at least; it was like we both had aged. "Jed!" she breathed.

"Hey, Laura," I said. And began to cry.

The students fell silent as they watched me; from the doorway the teacher heard the silence, looked over her shoulder—and freaked. She hurried to the her desk phone, punched a couple of numbers, and said urgently, "Principal to Mrs. Johnson's room—code thirteen."

Code 13. Let me guess: Crazed intruder? Unarmed loser? Nutcase from another town?

"It's okay, Mrs. Johnson, I know him!" Laura called, and hustled me out before the authorities came.

In the Camaro, I tried to get a grip. Laura sat with me in the big front seat and held the back of my neck like I was dog having a vomiting fit. I'm not quite sure why I was crying, but it couldn't have been more stupid or embarrassing.

"Hey, hey, it's gonna be all right," Laura said.

"Jesus, sorry," I mumbled. I couldn't look at her; I looked away, across the parking lot.

"Don't worry about it," she said.

After I had wiped my eyes, I managed to look sideways at her.

"What happened?" she asked. "Why are you here? Cool car, by the way."

I laughed once. Which is way better than crying, but similar in some ways. "All car and no life. To start, I've been kicked out of school."

"Jed!" was all she could say.

So I told her the story about surprising her sister on the back porch, about pocketing the joint, about forgetting it was there what with all the other shit happening—and then being busted. Her expression went from stunned, to furious with her sister, to silence, to an odd laugh.

"I'm sorry," she said quickly.

"It is kind of funny," I said with a shrug.

"No it isn't!" she said—and laughed again.

Soon we were both laughing hysterically. It felt good. It felt great.

"So, having nothing better to do," I continued, "I thought I'd go have a heart-to-heart with my dad at his motel. Except that he was there, screwing your mother."

Laura drew back; her face went pale.

"No, wait! I didn't mean to say it like that."

She stared at me. I thought she was going to bolt from car; that I'd never see her again.

"I'm sorry. I swear I didn't come up here to hurt you," I said. "It's just that I . . . couldn't think of anywhere else to go."

Then she began to cry. And how the next thing happened I don't know, but suddenly we were holding each other like we both were drowning. I buried my face in her hair, and she gripped me hard. I could feel her body convulsing as she cried, and I just hung on to her and kept stroking her golden hair. We stayed that way for long minutes, until she finally got a grip.

"I'm really sorry," she said, trying not to blubber. "I hardly ever cry."

"Look at it this way: At least you didn't break down in a classroom full of strangers."

She laughed once at this and turned her face to mine. I lifted my hand to wipe her tears; she clasped my fingers, pressed them tightly to her face. Her eyes were suddenly scared—as if her whole life were unraveling—and then we kissed.

We kissed hard—crazy hard—crushing our mouths against each other, pushing away any space between us, squeezing each other as if trying to hurt each other. I felt her teeth jar against mine, tasted her lip gloss, heard her whimper—and across the school parking lot a bell rang.

We pushed each other away at the same moment; we stared at each other, stunned. Time hung suspended; all clocks stopped

"What was that?" I said stupidly; I did not mean the school bell.

Laura touched her lips, her face, as if they were not her own. "I don't know."

I had no reply either. My mouth hung open.

"We must be crazy," she whispered.

We were silent; it was like the whole world had paused to listen for what came next.

"It's their fault," she said, suddenly angry.

"Whose fault?"

"Our parents', don't you see?" she said, her eyes blinking rapidly, her brain a processor trying to make sense of what just happened. "Their craziness—it got inside us."

"Shhhhh," I said. I reached over and touched her lips to stop the gush of words. And she clutched my hand, then pulled us together again. We didn't kiss this time, but just held each other.

"We're just confused, is all," she whispered, as if to herself. "We're both very vulnerable right now."

"Maybe," I said, and stroked her hair.

Wrong move.

"Don't!" she said, jerking back as if burned. Suddenly she was the old Laura, the former Laura, the in-full-command-of-my-life Laura. "We need to just forget that happened. Okay?"

I shrugged. "Okay. Sure," I said, trying to muster at least a little of the formerly cool Jed Berg. I checked my watch.

"Yes, you'd better get back to Duluth," she said. "You're in enough trouble for one day." She tried a smile that didn't quite work.

"No kidding," I said. "Though you're not exactly on time for English class."

"Mrs. Johnson is cool. She also knows about my parents' breakup; she'll be nice to me." Her eye contact was sketchy, her voice artificial, evasive.

"Well, then," I said, "I'd better go."

"Yes. For sure." She slid out of the Camaro.

I started the engine. "By the way, how's your crazy little sister doing?" I asked through my open window. Not that I cared; I only wanted to prolong this moment.

"Not good."

I looked up at her. I wanted to say more. About everything. About us. . . .

Laura touched my arm. "Go home, Jed," she said softly.

"I'm outa here," I said, and put the car in reverse.

In the mirror I watched her move quickly toward the school, her brown legs shining in the sunlight. At the door she turned to look back, then her yellow hair flashed as she disappeared inside the school.

As I left Ely, driving well below the speed limit, I felt out of body, surreal. I kept remembering Laura's body against mine, smelling her perfume, feeling the smooth rope of her hair, tasting her lip gloss. Laura, the girl who pissed me off more than anyone I'd met in years—how was it possible that we had kissed? She had to be right about the weird psychological state that we were in.

I drove on, replaying the scene in my head. Images of her

carried me through the forest, past the gnarled and stunted trees growing from crevices in the Shield, along the fence-like spires of black spruce and the unending, silent bogs. Thinking of her, unable to forget the hard swells of her body against mine, I drove all the way home.

Where my father was waiting.

In the Explorer on the street outside our house.

Strangely, I didn't mind. I could handle this. I parked and got out. He got out too.

"Jed," was all he said. Nothing about me driving the Camaro. He looked older, too, and clearly wanted to hug me but didn't. Actually I wouldn't have minded. The memory of kissing Laura was like a painkiller; everything had softer edges.

"Hey," I said.

"Listen," he began.

I did. I wasn't angry.

"You shouldn't have had to . . . experience that."

I waited.

"At the motel," he said.

I shrugged. The harder, sharper lines of my life ratcheted into focus, began to close in.

"Dr. Sanborn came down to talk about things . . . about what to do now, what comes next," he said. "That was all. And, well . . ."

I shrugged ever so slightly.

"But we don't need to go there," he said.

"Thank you," I said.

"Actually, the what-comes-next, that's what I need to talk to you about," he said.

I nodded.

"You want to . . . ?" He motioned to his Ford.

Actually, I preferred not to sit inside. It was like I would lose something: my independence, my mojo. The one Laura had given me. "Here is fine," I said. As a small gesture, I leaned against the fender of the Camaro. He followed suit.

He took a breath. "The upshot of it is, your mother and I . . . well, I don't think we're going to make it through this. As a couple, I mean."

I was silent. High above us, seagulls wheeled with faint shrieking calls.

"I can't tell you how sorry I am about this."

I looked at him.

"Did you hear what I'm saying?" he said.

"Yeah. Sure," I said.

There was a pause. "You're probably wondering why," he began.

Not really. . . . I looked beyond him, far out into the lake.

"It's hard to explain," he began. "Your mother is a remark-able, wonderful woman in many ways, but something went missing between us. Something I can't put my finger on. Something I still can't name. Anyway, it happened slowly, over a long period of time. She felt it too, I know. Then I met Dr. Sanborn. And, well, I suddenly saw how much was lost between your mother and me." He swallowed and paused.

I nodded ever so slightly; it was the least I could do. And the most.

"The same thing had happened with the Sanborns' marriage," he finished. "They thought building a new house might fix things. But it didn't. And well, here we are."

"So are you and Dr. Sanborn going to get married?" I asked. I looked directly at him. "Remarried, I mean?"

He looked away, off across the bay. "Probably. But not right away," he added quickly.

I was silent.

"And what about us kids? And the Sanborn kids?"

He swallowed. "Things . . . can work out."

I was silent for a moment. "And Mom?" I asked. "What about her?" My voice was suddenly louder.

He was silent. His Adam's apple bobbed, and there was sudden glistening in his eyes. "Your mother has many resources, friends and professionals, to help get her through this. She's a strong, intelligent woman."

We were both silent at that.

"Okay, then," I said, and stepped away from the car.

He remained leaning against the Camaro; he looked at me quizzically.

"Are you all right, Jed?" *That classic line from the soap operas, the one that means the screenwriter has come up empty: Are you all right?*

"Yes, I am," I said. "For the moment."

His eyes scanned me up and down; it was a good answer. He nodded. Suddenly he glanced up at the sun, then checked his wristwatch. "Say—shouldn't you be at tennis?" he asked.

"Yes, I should be," I said. I didn't want to complicate the moment, so didn't go into it. "In fact, I'd better get going."

"Okay, Jed."

We didn't hug or shake hands or anything—I couldn't touch him, and he seemed to understand this—so we parted. I headed into the house and didn't look back.

CHAPTER SIXTEEN

My mother worked late, so I cooked dinner for her. Spaghetti, green salad, garlic toast, a glass of red wine (for her). It was a meal my father had taught me how to cook, and I was rattling pans when she came through the front door.

She drew up to stare.

"Sorry about the mess," I said. The kitchen looked like I'd had a major party.

"No, it's fine. Thanks for cooking."

"I kinda thought you might need a good meal tonight," I said. There are lots of ways to apologize without using words, but this wasn't one of them. I didn't really think I had anything to apologize for. I just wanted to to do something nice for her.

She came quickly across the kitchen and hugged me from behind. Which was cool; my hands were busy cooking, and I briefly leaned back against her in acknowledgment, then continued playing chef.

"Jed, you didn't have to."

"Hey, I'll live."

"This is great. I'll get changed," she said, heading upstairs.

"Another five minutes, max," I called after her. Over my shoulder I watched her go. Weird not having my father around; I kind of felt like I was him. Like I was half son, half husband.

At dinner we were both hungry.

"Hope you didn't get in trouble from the judge, today," I ventured.

"It worked out," she said. "Plenty of cases ready to go. I just took a later slot."

I nodded.

She reached for more garlic toast. "And Monday we get things sorted out with you and school."

"Monday?" I said quickly.

"I got a call. We meet with the school judicial conduct board at eleven A.M."

I dropped my head. Stared at my plate.

"So tell me about the marijuana," she said.

I looked up at her. "I found it."

"Found it," she replied.

"One joint, lying on the ground."

She pursed her lips and stared back at me.

"Honestly," I said.

"All right. I believe you. So what were you going to do with it?"

"I don't know. Honestly."

After a long moment, she nodded. We resumed eating. Soon enough she said, "Did you talk with your father today?"

I nodded.

"And?"

"And what?" I said instantly; the hard, cold part of me stepped forward.

"About school. What we should do."

I shrugged. "No. It was more about . . . the future."

"Whose future?" There was sudden anger in her voice.

"Mainly his," I said.

"Well I have one too!" she said, turning to look out the window.

As do I, dammit. But in my best move of the day (aside from kissing Laura), I said nothing.

"Sorry, Jed," my mother said at length.

I shrugged. We finished dinner mostly in silence—it was clear we'd both had enough for today—and then she helped me tidy up the kitchen. Afterward we hung out in the den and watched *Wheel of Fortune*. She could always guess the words and phrases well before the contestants—though I wasn't so bad myself. We actually had a couple of laughs trying to beat each other. After Pat and Vanna, I flipped among several bad television movies without settling on any one in particular. This usually annoyed my mother—me not settling on one program and sticking with it—but tonight she said nothing. Which, go figure, made me understand how totally annoying channel surfing had to be for the person without the remote. I locked into a bug-and-monkey nature show, the one where the narrator's voice is better than a sleeping pill, and set the remote aside.

"Remember, when I was small, that happy little painter guy?" I asked. "The one who did a whole painting while you watched?"

"Bob Ross," she said.

"I always liked him," I said.

"Me too," she said. "His show was the only way I could get you to lie down and maybe take a nap."

We watched some monkeys chatter and hoot at a passing snake. "He died not too long ago. Did you know that?" I said.

My mother looked startled. "No. I didn't hear that."

I didn't know why I'd brought that up, so I watched the nature show in silence. Then I heard her sniffling softly. I looked over.

"I'm sorry," she said. She was wiping her eyes.

"It's all right."

"No it's not. It's been a long day, I guess. I should go to bed."

I nodded.

She kissed the top of my head as she left the room "See you in the morning, Jed-eye. Lock up the house, please."

Then it was just me downstairs. After a while I got up and went into the living room; I looked about at the wide windows, the various doors. It was a strange feeling without my dad around. Quietly I stepped outside onto the front porch and scanned the neighborhood. The tidy wide yards were empty, the houses quiet and far below; the yellow lights of the lift bridge stood squarely in place. No bad guys in sight. I locked the doors and window latches, then headed upstairs to check my e-mail before bed.

Hi Jed,

You've probably heard the good news by now. My mother is talking divorce. "I thought it was important to be up-front," she said. "To let everybody know where they stand." "Gee, thanks," I told her. And things went downhill from there. Jenny went berserk. Jenny, who hates everything, including me, my parents, the house and town we live in--she's the one who can't deal with it. Go figure. She went totally out of control, screamed at my mother, tried to hit her, broke two lamps. We had to wrestle her to the floor. She even bit my mother. It was crazy--like she was wild animal. My mother gave her a pill of some kind to make her relax and sleep. It took a while, but she finally calmed down. I think she should be in the hospital or some place like that. She's totally screwed up, has been for a long time, but this really put her over the top now. My mother feels terrible about Jenny. "What did you expect?" I told her. And then she fell apart at that and cried for an hour at least. It was cruel of me, but I feel cruel right now. I don't much care about Jenny even. She's always made trouble for our family (maybe in some

unconscious way my mother is trying to escape from Jenny--
high school is going to be hell for her). I've always been the one
to keep Jenny in line, and make sure she doesn't get too crazy.
And she's always hated me anyway. Explain that to me. Guess
it's why I like being alone in my kayak.
Sorry, this is too long but I had to tell someone who isn't a
friend--shit, you know what I mean--someone not in my
hometown. Hope you're doing all right. . . . BTW, I'm sorry
about today, you know, in the car.
L

Laura
Yes, I got the same bad news from my father when I got home.
They must have coordinated it. What can I say?
About Jenny--geez, I didn't know she was that nutty. But you're not
her mother. I don't mean to be cold here, hope you understand. The
car thing? I don't know what to say. It felt really good, kissing you.
If it never happens again, I guess I can live with that. But it's not
something I will ever forget.
Good night.
J
P.S. Wish me luck on Monday. I meet with the school goons at
11 a.m., about my drug addiction.

After I hit Send, I sat for a couple minutes in hope of a
reply. There was none.

CHAPTER SEVENTEEN

The weekend, to borrow a phrase, looked like a bust. Now that I was formally a doper, my friends sounded odd on the phone; some didn't return my calls, or were "busy" when their parents answered. News travels fast. I didn't bother to call Cassie. Word was she had rebounded nicely with some football player, who was taking her to the prom. As a last resort, there was Bobby—but then I remembered that he was gone with the tennis team. So I stayed home Saturday night and made a show of doing "schoolwork" on my computer—which became e-mail with Laura.

We stayed up almost all night, talking, and by Sunday we had told each other our life's story and then some. I hardly left my room. We made top-ten lists. We told all of our "firsts." Our most embarrassing moments (mine a seventh-grade costume party that wasn't a costume party; hers throwing up in the school pool during a swim meet). Our saddest kid-moments (Laura finding her entire collection of unicorn figures smashed, of course by Jenny; mine being chosen last for a first-grade kick-ball team). Our worst teenage moments (mine a boil on my nose the size of a mushroom on the first day of ninth grade; hers a favorite uncle who touched her breast). We told each other everything.

But suddenly it was Monday. I awoke to find my mother looming over my bed. "Whoa!" I said, bunching my blankets about my waist; I'd been dreaming of Laura, and I hoped it wasn't obvious.

"Sorry, Jed. I knocked on the door but you were dead to the world." She kept her gaze tastefully above my shoulders.

"What time is it?" I mumbled. She was all dressed for work.

"Seven thirty. Remember—we meet with the school judicial conduct board at eleven A.M."

"Yeah, like I've forgotten." Though actually, for parts of the weekend, I had.

"Just making sure." She turned to go.

"So what do I have to do at his meeting?" I said.

"Just be there. Explain yourself honestly. We'll get it over and done with and try to get you back on track with school, tennis, your old life." Her voice was calculatedly cheerful.

"My old life? Yeah, sure," I said.

"Anyway," she said briskly, checking her watch, "I'll meet you at my office at ten forty-five. Sharp. Okay?"

I was silent. Then nodded.

"You want me to come get you?" she said, narrowing her eyes.

"What—you think I'm not going to show?"

"No. Well, honestly?"

"Yes."

"People have done stupider things."

"Hey, I want to get this over with too."

"Good. And one last thing: Maybe dress up a bit?"

I stared at her. "What, like a suit and tie? Like I'm on Court TV or something?"

"No—just decent khakis, a nice shirt, that sort of thing."

"Sure, counselor. Whatever you say."

She drew back, hurt. "Ten forty-five."

"Okay, okay!"

"I set the oven timer in the kitchen for ten o'clock—in case you fall back asleep," she said.

"Sleep, right," I muttered after her. I lay there for a while, staring at the ceiling, listening to her feet go down the stairs, to the garage door opening and closing, to her car receding down the street. I closed my eyes and tried to bring back my dream of Laura—we were floating down a river on some kind of picnic table—but the dream was crowded out by images of detention monitor Mr. Thompson glaring down at me from a giant elevated desk.

Still in bed, I flipped on my TV. Local Duluth-area news.

"In weather, a strong line of low pressure in North Dakota is poised to push through north-central Minnesota later today, creating conditions for afternoon thunderstorms, some severe. . . ."

I skipped through the channels, past the cheerful, out-going, start-your-day-with-us type newscasters, each pretending to be interested in a second-rate author, or a dog trainer and his mutt, or a master gardener with tips on growing giant marigolds. Morning television was hell. Then the phone rang—probably my mother reminding me to wear a tie.

"Jed?"

"Laura!"

She laughed at my surprise. "Yes."

"Are you all right?"

"Sure, how about you? Still in bed?" She was even more cheerful sounding than my mother.

"Yes."

"So what time is your school judicial thing again?"

"Eleven."

"Perfect," she said.

"Perfect for what?"

"For me to be there. I'm just getting ready to leave Ely."

"You're coming to my judicial conduct meeting?"

"Hey, it's the least I can do. Two hours from now is ten A.M.

We'll have time for breakfast, then we'll do the meeting."

"Why would you want to be at that meeting?"

"First, to tell them exactly where the marijuana came from. How it's not really your fault, blah, blah, blah. Laura Sanborn, 'All-American,' takes the stand on your behalf."

"Great," I said. "And the second reason?"

There was silence. "Just because I want to," she said softly.

I fought back the urge to blurt out something stupid.

"Perkins at ten?" she asked.

"I'm already there. Eating pancakes," I said.

She laughed and we hung up.

I waited nervously at Perkins, sitting so I could see the highway, but somehow I missed her car, because suddenly a flash of bright-pink hair came through the doorway.

"Very funny," I called across the restaurant.

Her laugh carried to every table in the place; all eyes turned. "Hi, Jed," she said. We hugged—awkwardly—and then she plopped into the booth.

We sat there grinning at each other. "Just what I need— a character witness with pink hair," I began.

She laughed again, then stripped off her wig and fluffed her real, golden ponytail. "I thought a little humor might be in order."

Her scent, her teeth, her skin, her dancing eyes left me

dumb. "How'd you . . . get out of school?" I said stupidly.

"Actually, I'm supposed to be home baby-sitting Jenny."

"Why's she home?"

"Too nutty for school right now," Laura said. "She's on some meds my mother gave her, and she'll sleep until noon at least." She quickly checked her watch. "So hey, here I am."

"Thanks," I said.

She shrugged. "That's what people do, yes? Help each other."

I tried for a smile but failed: She helped people; I mainly looked out for myself.

She slid her tanned fingers across the table and touched mine. "So what do we do?" she asked. There was an urgency in her voice.

"About what?"

"About our parents. About . . . everything."

Then, in either perfect or perfectly horrible timing, the waitress arrived. "Do you know what you want?" she asked brightly.

Laura and I looked at each other; we began to laugh wildly.

"I'll give you a couple of minutes," the waitress said, turning away.

"No, wait, we're sorry," Laura called to her.

The waitress returned and gave us a second chance. When she left, we began to giggle again.

"Have you ever noticed how waitpeople always arrive during life-defining moments?" I said. I was prepared to laugh in the old Jed Berg style, but Laura didn't follow my lead.

"That's what this feels like to you?"

I swallowed. "God, I hope my parents don't do it," I blurted. Suddenly my eyes were burning. It was the first time I'd said it out loud: I did *not* want my parents to divorce.

"But it might happen, Jed," she said quietly. "Probably will happen."

I wiped my eyes angrily. "And then what?"

"Well," she began, searching for words, "I suppose if my mother marries your father, we'd sort of be family."

"I don't want to be family with you."

She stared at me.

With good timing, the waitress arrived with our orange juice, and soon enough our cakes came. Gradually the mood lightened. Maybe it was the pancake-syrup sugar buzz, maybe it was just being together, but for a half hour we talked and laughed and teased each other and ate pancakes as if life were good, as if the world were perfect and we could not be touched by it—until her cell phone beeped.

She hurriedly dug in her purse, put the little phone to her

ear. "Jenny!" Laura said. Her eyes widened.

I looked up; I carefully put down my fork.

"What are you talking about? Don't be crazy," Laura said. "I'll be home soon—very soon."

I frowned, puzzled.

"Jenny, listen to me!" Laura said loudly. Then she swore and put down the phone. She looked at me. Her face was splotchy with anger. "She hasn't been taking her meds, and she just called to tell me that our family is crazy and she's running away to Canada to find a new one."

"Canada?"

"Not running away, actually. Paddling away. In my kayak. She's heading into the BWCAW."

I was silent. Canada was actually not that far; the lakes were all connected. "Why would she do that?" I asked.

"Because she's crazy. Because it's something to draw maximum attention to herself. Because it's something to cause more trouble for our family," Laura said in a rush. She swore again, then stared out the window.

"She won't do it."

"She will, she is," Laura said instantly. "You don't know her. She was already in the car. She hangs out with these older kids and gets rides from them."

I was silent.

"And the thing of it is, she doesn't know anything about the

BWCAW. The water is cold; the ice has been out for barely three weeks." Laura's voice tilted from anger toward fear.

"So we go after her," I said.

"We?"

"You and me. I've been in the BWCAW lots of times with my father. I've got a J-stroke you wouldn't believe."

"You've also got a judicial hearing."

I fell silent. "Shit," I said.

Laura stared at me. "This is terrible," she murmured. She looked at her watch.

I drummed my fingers rapidly. "Do you know where she'd go, where she'd launch?"

"There's only one spot that she knows—the place I took her. It's actually southeast of Ely, on White Iron lake." Laura looked at me, and again at her watch.

"Is she any good paddling?"

"She's skinny and scrawny, but yeah, she can paddle. I taught her."

"How far southeast of Ely is White Iron Lake?"

"Twenty minutes or so."

I thought it through. "If you have to drive all the way home, get your gear, then come back, she'll have a major head start," I said.

Laura swallowed. "I could call my parents. The police even. Just what our family needs right now—more trouble."

Tears welled in her eyes.

"Hey, your parents don't need to know about this. We'll go from here. We'll take my Dad's Wenonah. What gear we need. We'll catch up with her and get her home, and no one will be the wiser."

"But Jed, your school conduct meeting."

I swallowed. "I think—I hope—my mother can cover for me. And anyway, if Jenny is as crazy as you say, you'll need someone to help."

Laura reached over and touched my face. Which, I realized, was all I really wanted.

CHAPTER EIGHTEEN

At my house we threw the Wenonah on top of the Honda and some day-trip gear in a Duluth pack.

"Tent? Bags?" Laura said.

I looked up. "Hey, we'll be in and out in a few hours."

"There might be some weather," she said. "It's spring—you never know."

"You're right." I grabbed a couple of sleeping bags, a tent, some rain gear, the little propane stove, some food pouches, canteen, matches. All went into the familiar green Duluth pack, the one my father always used.

"Binoculars?" Laura asked.

"There," I said, pointing to a shelf, and within ten minutes we were speeding up Highway 61. Laura led the way in her car, driving like a maniac. I had my story (*life and death, officer*) at the tip of my tongue, but the highway gods were with us: not a patrol car in sight the whole trip. I followed Laura's car off the blacktopped highway, down a narrow gravel road—then braked when she did. An old Ford sedan, with kids covering it like pigeons on a park bench, sat at the landing; as we came fast around the bend, the kids leaped off and pitched beer cans into the woods.

Laura quickly got out of her car and confronted the school skippers. "So where's Jenny?"

"Jenny who?" a spiky-haired boy with a goatee said; the others looked over their shoulders, toward the lake.

"She, like, took off," a girl said, nodding toward the water.

"Where?"

The motley bunch looked nervously at each other. "She said your family had this cabin on this island, that we could party there," one of them said. "She's supposed to come back and get us."

"And how would you all get to the island in one kayak?" Laura said.

The losers looked at each other.

"She's running away, you idiots—to Canada. And you helped her."

"Shit, man," one of them murmured.

"We're wasting time," Laura said to me, but I was already unstrapping the canoe. She looked across the lake. "How long has she been gone?"

The older guy with the wispy goatee shrugged. "I dunno. We kinda lost track of time."

One of them giggled.

Laura picked up a canoe paddle.

"An hour. No more than that," a skinny punk girl said quickly.

Laura said to me, "About what we thought." She turned to the others. "Why don't you all get lost? Like go find some friends your own age?"

Muttering, the gang piled into their car; the driver spun the tires as they raced off.

I had the gear mostly unloaded by then, and only minutes later we launched. I took the bow. Laura, with our gear toward the stern, outbalanced my weight—actually, she probably didn't weigh that much less than me—but in any case she needed to steer: She knew where we were going.

"Nice paddle," Laura said as we readied ourselves.

I hoisted the bent-shaft, laminated Grey Owl, made in Canada. With its alternating pale and dark stripes sealed under a clear, shiny coat of spar varnish, it was a handsome piece of wood. "It's my father's."

Laura was silent.

We set off across the wine-dark water at a killer pace: about a dozen hard strokes, then "Hup!" from Laura, the traditional signal to switch sides with our paddles. At first we were stiff and clumsy in our crossovers; soon, however, our blades flashed overhead like cheerleading batons arcing left, then right, left, then right. White Iron Lake, stretching northeast, was long and narrow and boatless; this was the middle of the week, and the fishing season had not begun. Our bad luck.

Laura was reading my mind. "A motorboat wouldn't help us. Just ahead, when White Iron turns into the Kawishiwi River, we're in the BWCAW. No motorboats allowed."

I nodded and kept paddling.

"She has an hour's head start. At least," Laura said from behind me. She wore the binoculars around her neck.

"But we're going twice as fast."

"Don't bet on it," Laura said.

"If Train A leaves the station at eleven A.M., traveling east at two miles per hour, and Train B leaves the same station at noon, traveling three miles per hour . . ."

"How long does it take for Train B to catch up with Train A?" Laura finished.

"I don't know. I never could do those math problems," I replied. All I remembered was that it would take Train B a surprisingly long time to catch up—but this I didn't mention.

"Actually, using your numbers, about two hours," Laura said.

Of course she would know the formula.

We concentrated upon muscling our way up the empty, tree-lined river. The Wenonah, which weighed less than thirty pounds, left a fine, flat wake that curved in on itself in rust-colored fingers of foam. God bless geeky scientists. The Kevlar fabric, the same material used in bulletproof vests, was lightweight, flexible, rockproof, and it floated us like a leaf—a leaf helped along by a steady tail breeze.

I looked again over my shoulder at the color of the sky. Make that noncolor.

Laura, too, glanced back. "Some weather for sure," she said.

"We've got hours before that stuff arrives. We'll have Jenny back at the landing and under house arrest by then." I was finding my role: the canoe's optimist.

"Keep looking onshore in case she gave up and pulled in," Laura called, scanning the water with the glasses.

I nodded; I'd already thought of that, but so far all we'd seen were loons, a couple of dark, immature eagles, plus an osprey with a fish gripped like a torpedo in its claws.

An hour later, our crossover changes began to falter, and I could hear Laura breathing as hard as I was. "Gorp?" she called.

"Thought you'd never ask." I drew in my paddle and we coasted. Though the sun had gone behind clouds, and the wind was cooler now, I stripped off my shirt. Panting, I tipped backward and looked at Laura upside down. She had peeled off her sweatshirt and now wore just a black sports bra; down its front was a darker V of sweat. Her breasts pushed against the fabric, and her nipples were stiff from the chill off the water.

"That was a good push," she said with a smile.

"Thanks." I was too out of breath to say more. I caught the bag of raisins, oil seeds, peanuts, and M&M's, and poured a full handful in my mouth. Took a drink from the canteen. Took some downtime.

After about thirty seconds, Laura said, "Sorry, Jed, but we'd better keep moving or we'll never get there."

I sat up and dug back in. But "there" kept unwinding ahead of us. We stroked hard and fast. With the binoculars Laura scanned the river in front of us, but no Jenny. Behind us in the west, clouds rolled up higher and grayer.

"Might get a little rain later," I said cheerfully. *As in a lot of rain, and wind, too.* We both wore our sweatshirts now; the temperature had dropped several degrees.

"Not good," Laura said of the sky.

We pushed on. Around every bend we both leaned forward expecting to see a flash of yellow kayak, but nothing—until an oncoming canoe appeared.

"Hullo!" Laura called, and held up her paddle. We steered quickly their way.

"Hey," said a scruffy fellow in the stern. Two guys in their twenties, several days' beard, lots of gear. We closed fast.

"Everything okay?" the bow paddler asked.

"Have you seen a girl in a yellow kayak?" Laura asked. "Heading upriver?"

The guys looked at each other and laughed. "With green hair?"

"Yes," Laura said.

"We passed right by her. Looked like she was struggling, tired or something. So we stopped and asked if she needed help."

"And she probably flipped you off," Laura finished.

"You must know her pretty well," the guy in the stern said.

"My sister," Laura said.

"She in trouble of some kind?" the bow man asked.

"Something like that," Laura said, checking her watch.

"You need help?" he added.

His partner said quickly, "Hey, she's less than a mile ahead of you and not going very fast. A half hour, max, you've got her."

Laura glanced at me. "She's slowed way down."

The bow paddler said, "We'll help you if you really need it."

"They'll be fine!" the stern man said. "Sorry," he added, turning to us. "We've been in the bush a couple of weeks and our car's only a couple of hours away, plus we don't want to get wet." He glanced skyward and shrugged. "You know how it is."

"Sure," I answered.

"You guys got rain gear, tent, everything you need?" the bow paddler asked.

"Got it covered," Laura said shortly, and with a powerful stroke pushed us away and upstream. As the other canoe passed and moved downriver, we could hear the men arguing.

I concentrated upon paddling hard in order to keep her long strokes from angling us first left, then right.

At about three thirty in the afternoon we spotted her.

"There she blows!" I called out.

"Shhhh!" Laura said instantly, raising the binoculars to squint past me. "Don't scare her."

"So we sneak up on her?"

"Sort of. I don't want to totally surprise her. Have her do something stupid."

I nodded and concentrated on making no splashes with my paddle, no clunk of wood against the gunwale. We closed from a quarter mile to a hundred yards. Jenny's green hair was a like a beacon. She was laboring—bent at the waist, dragging her blade forward across the small chop instead of lifting it, and the kayak moved jerkily forward with a side-to-side, crablike motion.

"She's done for the day," Laura breathed as we watched her struggle.

It was definitely a pathetic sight.

"Get ready," Laura said. I heard her life vest clips snap softly into place. Turning, I saw that she had peeled off her big sweatshirt and was ready to get wet if necessary. "Jenny!" Laura called.

Jenny whirled as if shot at; she stared, then paddled madly in the opposite direction.

"Yes, go to shore. We've got food and water," Laura called.

At the word *shore*, Jenny reversed direction and headed toward the widest part of the river.

"Shit," Laura muttered. "We have to cut her off."

"Leave me alone," Jenny cried. "Just leave me alone."

"We will," Laura called. "But we have to get to shore. There's a storm coming, and I know you're hungry and tired."

"I'm going to Canada," Jenny said. "People are less crazy there."

"People are crazy everywhere, plus Canada is still thirty miles ahead."

Jenny slumped over and coasted. We closed to within a few yards. She looked as bedraggled as a baby raccoon clinging to a floating log.

She fastened her eyes on me. "Who's he?" she said with sudden alarm.

"This is . . . Jed," Laura said.

Jenny gave me a second, closer look.

"You!" she cried. "You were the Domino's guy, spying on us, just like your father!" She hurled her paddle, which caught me off guard—and squarely across the forehead. A burning sparkle of lights flashed between my eyes and I jerked backward. I heard Laura shout. Heard a splash. When I sat up, my yellow stars merged with the yellow of the kayak—which was was upside down. Only a second or two had passed, but Jenny was underwater and Laura was in midair.

She splashed down hard but popped up as if the cold water had flung her upward. "Jed, get closer with the canoe!" She bobbed now in her life jacket. Something was running into my eye, but I wiped it with the back of my hand and pushed forward toward the kayak. Laura heaved herself up, straddled the kayak, clenched her legs around it like a bronco rider, and rolled sideways. In her scissors grip, the kayak rotated and Jenny appeared coughing and spitting.

"God, this water!" Laura said as she surfaced. "Okay, Jed. You got to get us to shore. Now. Oh, Jesus, look at your face."

I could see blood on my hand and arm.

"I'm okay," I said. "Hold on to the stern—I'll tow you."

I scooted mid canoe, got onto my knees, and began to paddle like a voyageur.

"This water is so cold!" Laura repeated.

The shore was a only a couple of hundred yards away, but the weight of Laura in the water towing the kayak behind her made it slow going—too slow.

"Get up on the kayak, at least partway," I called.

"Okay." I heard her scrambling and splashing "Help me, dammit," Laura said. Jenny reached out a skinny arm, which was just enough for Laura to heave herself mostly aboard.

"Great, much better!" I shouted.

"Someday," Laura said, glowering at her sister; Jenny had begun to shiver uncontrollably.

"Save it," I said. "Just hang on. We're almost there."

In under ten minutes I drove the canoe hard onto a flat, smooth plate of gray Canadian Shield. I leaped out into the shallow water—was stunned at the fiery coldness of the water in my boots—and pulled Laura forward onto dry rock, then grabbed Jenny and hoisted her out of the kayak. Her lips were blue tinged, and she was still shuddering uncontrollably.

Onshore, our troubles were not over. "We need a fire, as in now," I said. "Where are those matches?"

Laura hoisted herself onto her knees; her arms had patches of bluish skin. "In here," she said, her teeth chattering. She tried to unbuckle the Duluth pack straps but couldn't manage.

"I'll do it," I said.

"Sorry. My hands are kind of numb. My legs, too." A tremor shot through her. She crawled across the smooth stone to Jenny.

I wiped my face again—my chest was spotted with blood—and pulled the canoe farther onshore so I could rummage through the pack. "Got 'em!" I said.

"Good. But first—and I really hate to do this to you—" Laura said—she actually laughed, along with a shudder of cold, "can you hand me that sleeping bag? I need to be in it, along with Jenny."

I looked at Jenny, whose eyes were glazed and dull.

"I'm on it," I said.

I worked fast. I found the bag and a sleeping mat, then helped Laura take off Jenny's boots and peel off her shorts, panties, and sports bra. It was like I was a nurse or an EMT; the clock was ticking, though mostly for Jenny. She shuddered continuously. I manhandled her into the bag—she could only glare, her arms too cold to flail at me, her legs too stiff to kick—and within a couple of minutes I had both sisters zipped in snugly. Laura's arms were wrapped tightly around Jenny.

"We-we're good now," Laura said. "Ab-about that fire?"

"Hey, no problem. This is not a Jack London story, all right?"

"Cool," she said, mustering a little smile.

"Give me five minutes and I'll have some major heat. I'll be just beyond this outcropping of rocks."

She nodded; I got busy. I didn't have a hatchet, but there was plenty of dry bark and tinder at the edge of the forest. Thank God it hadn't rained for a few days.

There was no drama to building the fire; I arranged a tiny tepee of dried tree moss, spruce twigs, and dead leaves, which flared up yellow with one match. I carefully layered on a dozen finger-thick sticks. All good. When I was sure the fire was going, I stepped farther back and began ripping off branches from a downed tree. When the fire was secure, I stepped back over the outcropping to look down at the sisters.

"I see smoke," Laura said. Jenny was looking around as well, though she still had a glassy stare.

"As in fire," I said.

"I knew you were hot," she said.

"Lame joke," I answered.

And then a phone rang.

At first I thought it was some kind of forest bird: *chirp, chirp chirp*.

Laura was confused as well. We both looked around.

"My cell, Jed! It's in the Duluth pack—in a plastic bag."

I hopped down, hurdled a scrubby spruce, and dug inside the pack. A phone in a Zip-lock, sure enough. I tore open the bag—for some reason it seemed important to take the call—and pressed the Speak button.

"Hello—who's this?" a woman's voice said.

"Ah, who's this?" I said dumbly. My head was beginning to ache and I could feel something crusty forming over my right eyebrow.

"Dr. Sanborn is who this is. Where's Laura?"

"One moment please," I answered in my best customer service voice. I stepped over to the sleeping bag. "It's your mother."

Laura's eyes widened; she reached for the phone.

"Yes, Jenny's here with me," Laura said immediately, looking sideways at her sister; I watched as Laura listened. "No, we're fine. Fine. Yeah, why wouldn't we be fine?" She shivered.

I covered my mouth so as not to laugh.

"Who was that?" Laura asked. She looked at me. "That was . . . Jed Berg. As in son of Garrett Berg, the architect?"

There was some major dead air.

"Where are we? What's going on?" Laura repeated. She looked at me and shrugged. "Well, to be honest, the three of us are canoeing on the Kawishiwi."

A small screeching came from the phone, and I listened as Laura gradually explained herself—to the tune of more and louder screeching sounds.

"Yes, I know I'm supposed to be home . . ."

"Yes, I supposed I could have called you . . ."

"Jed? Because, unlike most adults lately, Jed's dependable—that's why. I also thought he was the best person to help," Laura said, anger in her voice.

Ouch.

"Listen—I wasn't the one who ran away," Laura added, casting her gaze sideways at Jenny. "Jed's become a . . . friend of mine; he also knows his way around a canoe."

More listening.

"Yes, I knew where'd she be . . . yes . . . yes."

"Where are we exactly?" Laura repeated. "Up the Kawishiwi a few miles. Where I took her that time, yes . . . Well, there's some weather coming in, so I think we'll camp here for tonight and come back first thing in the morning."

Dr. Sanborn's voice was suddenly audible; Laura held the phone away from her head.

"No, we're not going back onto the river. It's windy now, and it's going to rain, and this weather needs to pass."

"Yes. Yes. Yes. Yes, a rain fly. Everything we need, yes. Just relax, okay?"

More listening.

"Right now? Right now we're just about to sit down around a campfire. And have s'mores," Laura added.

I rolled my eyes; at least the first part was true.

"Yes, I'll call you. Of course, yes."

I signaled to Laura.

"Hold on just a sec."

I whispered to Laura; she paused, then nodded

"Would you do one thing?" she said into the phone. "Could you call Jed's mom?"

There was silence.

"So she knows where he is, that's why!" Laura answered. "He sort of missed an important meeting."

She turned to me. "My mother wants to know why can't you call her yourself?"

"Because she'll think I'm lying," I said.

"Because she'll think he's lying," Laura repeated into the phone. She listened.

"Well, we're already kinda connected, yes? As in two families, I mean. Not that that's *my* fault," Laura added.

I could tell that her body heat was coming back fast.

"Mother, it won't hurt you. Thanks. And Jed thanks you, too," she said. She listened. "Okay, okay. Yes, we'll be fine. Good-bye. Yes, I love you. No, don't worry about it. 'Bye."

With that the phone beeped. We looked at each other.

"Was that Mom?" Jenny said dully.

"Yes. Now go to sleep," Laura said.

"Okay," she murmured, and clutched her big sister tighter.

A few minutes later I had the fire blazing waist high—crackling and popping—and I didn't hear Laura behind me. Laura, her cold bare feet silent on the smooth and ancient stone; Laura, naked but for the canvas Duluth pack held more or less in front of her. "I hope you don't mind," she said, leaning close to the fire. "I need to get totally warm."

"You want me to leave?" I said dumbly.

"Not necessarily," she said. She turned her bare back to the fire. I stared at her for a long moment, then looked into the flames. "I'll start the s'mores now," I said.

She laughed, then turned her front to the heat.

"How many marshmallows would you like?" I asked, fitting an imaginary marshmallow onto an imaginary stick.

"Two, please," she said.

I held my hand toward the fire.

"Don't burn them!" she said.

I rotated my wrist. We both stared just beyond my fingertips.

"There we have it," I said, swinging my arm her way.

"Perfect," she said, and reached out to accept.

I let my eyes travel down her body. "Like you," I said softly.

"Ah, Jed? Maybe you should get my sweatshirt now?" She smiled shyly and hugged her arms across her chest.

"Sure."

At the canoe, I checked on Jenny. She was half sleeping, half shivering, not the best combination. "Hey, Jenny, wake up. I've got a fire going."

She managed to hoist one skinny middle finger.

"On the other hand, you're fine," I said. I brought Laura her clothes.

"Thanks, rescue guy," she said as she shrugged on her big sweatshirt. "You did all the right things."

"Get them naked, get them warm," I said. "Maybe it's a guy thing, but that's easy to remember."

She laughed, came over, and hugged me. "This is a part of warming up, too," she said, and gave me a quick kiss on the lips.

"I forgot the hugging part," I murmured into her still-wet hair.

We hung on to each other tightly.

I broke away first. "We probably should get wild child out of her sleeping bag and close to the fire. She's still got the shakes."

"You're right," Laura said, quickly all business.

"I'll go look for a better campsite," I said, glancing at the sky, "somewhere in the trees."

I followed an animal trail that paralleled the shore and then rose toward higher ground. Suddenly the trail widened, and all available downed firewood disappeared. Sure enough,

I walked into an empty campsite: fire ring, sitting logs, and two pressed-down tent areas on the pine-needled dirt.

"Excellent," I murmured. The pines around were massive—bigger in diameter than garbage cans—plus they sheltered the site from the west winds. I spent ten minutes foraging for firewood and soon had a nice pile—certainly enough to get us through the night. Which all in all had excellent possibilities.

CHAPTER NINETEEN

When I returned to the landing twenty minutes later, Jenny wore a rain poncho (only, I guessed) and squatted sullenly by the fire; her clothes steamed on a stick that she held over the flames.

"Keep moving them," Laura commanded as she sorted out the tent stakes and rain fly. "If they catch on fire, you have to go home naked."

Jenny shot me a dark look.

"Don't get too comfortable, gang," I announced. "There's a real campsite just ahead."

"Great!" Laura exclaimed.

"Why can't we stay here?" Jenny muttered.

"We'll need some protection from the weather, plus it's kind of hard to pound tent stakes into solid rock," Laura said.

She and I set about securing the kayak, then gathering up the gear. I hoisted the canoe, Laura the Duluth pack, and Jenny the armful of hot, damp clothes. The wind gusted beneath Jenny's poncho and for an instant revealed her skinny white butt. "Dammit!" she shouted; she whirled to glare at me with anger and shame.

I tried not to grin.

"Hey, it's nothing Jed hasn't seen," Laura remarked. "Who do you think got us naked and into the sleeping bag?"

"You probably liked it," Jenny muttered.

"Maybe I did," Laura shot back.

"Okay, okay, girls—let's go," I said. And we set off up the hill. Laura kept a hand on the stern of the canoe—the wind threatened to lift it off my shoulders and fling it back into the lake. On the Kawishiwi, whitecaps skittered along; across the wide river, pointed spruce tops on the far shore tilted ten degrees eastward and did not straighten. It was a steady blow.

"Great!" Laura said as we arrived at the campsite. "You even got a fire going."

"Not sure how long it will last if it rains, but why not?"

"We might get lucky," Laura said, dropping the gear.

Jenny straggled in and paused to look around at the site; she had nothing bad to say, which was a miracle.

"Help me with the tent," Laura ordered her.

As they worked, so did I. Using the heavy sitting logs, one of which showed some serious claw marks, I wedged the canoe upside down and turned the Wenonah into a low-angle lean-to. Securing it was no small measure of work, but I was not letting the canoe blow away. There was, after all, the small matter of getting back to Duluth tomorrow and facing my mother, which I quickly put out of my head.

When the tent, a sturdy two-person dome, was erect, Jenny immediately crawled inside and yanked shut the zipper. "Don't get too spread out—we all need to fit in there," Laura said.

I pointed to my lean-to canoe contraption. "I'll probably hunker down out here, keep an eye on things."

"Are you sure?"

I nodded.

"I'll come later and sit with you," Laura said.

"I'd like that," I said.

"God! Why don't you two just go out in the woods and have sex!" Jenny said from inside the tent.

"Hey!" Laura said angrily. "You want to sleep in the tent tonight or not? I'm telling you, if you piss me off any further, you're sleeping in the woods—you got that?"

From the tent there was loud silence.

Muttering, Laura tied down the last of the corner straps with double knots, and then there was nothing to do but wait.

Facing southeast, with a hillside behind and towering red pines all around, the campsite was perfectly positioned.

Laura and I hunkered down and fed the fire. Inside the tent, Jenny was quiet.

After a few minutes, Laura looked at me, then tiptoed to the east-facing door and peered inside a small opening in the zipper. "Sleeping," Laura mouthed

I smiled and beckoned her back to the fire. She settled down alongside me, and I put my arm around her and arranged the rain poncho over our legs.

"Mmmmm. This feels good," she said. I felt her muscles relax as she leaned against me. We sat that way for several minutes. Just when I had worked up the courage to kiss her, her eyelids drooped.

"Why don't you take a little nap?" I said.

"I couldn't," she murmured, and melted against me even as she spoke.

I held her. She fell asleep within a minute. With the fire snapping, and the wind coursing like a river through the treetops above us, I stroked Laura's hair while she slept. She began to snore lightly. Lesser, false epiphanies began to drift through my head—those stupid moments, like driving my father's Camaro and thinking my life could never get any better. . . .

I must have dozed—until somewhere behind us a treetop snapped with a whiplike pop. Laura flinched.

"It's okay, just a branch," I said. The wind was stronger

now, not gusts but a gradually rising speed as if someone, somewhere, were turning up a giant velocity dial.

"Must have dozed off," Laura mumbled, wiping her mouth.

"As in sawing logs," I said.

"Really?" She sat up. "I'm embarrassed."

"No, you were tired."

She touched my face. "How about you?"

I shrugged. "Keeper of the fire never sleeps."

She looked at the fire, now a dull bed of coals. "I'll put some wood on."

I watched her as she worked.

"What time is it?" Laura asked.

"Seven."

"We should eat supper before it starts to rain."

We set about boiling water for a pouch meal for four: Bandito Scramble, meaning eggs, rice, and a packet of salsa for flavor.

She woke Jenny. "I'm not eating that," Jenny said.

"Fine," Laura replied. "More for us."

She and I passed the pouch; Jenny tried to ignore us by looking at the fire.

"Okay, okay, I'll try some," Jenny said.

Laura gave her the remains, which Jenny wolfed down with no complaints. "There are some candy bars and water," Laura said. "But that's it for tonight."

"What about tomorrow?" Jenny said.

"When were you the one to ever ask about tomorrow?" Laura said.

Jenny lowered her head.

Laura watched her. "Sorry," she said at length.

Jenny shrugged.

"Tomorrow we have gorp and water for breakfast," Laura said. "Then we paddle home."

"I hate that kayak," Jenny said.

"We'll tow it. You can take the duffer seat in the canoe."

Jenny was silent. She poked at the fire. "I can help paddle too."

"Don't worry, kid, you'll get your turn," Laura said.

By seven thirty it was too dark and rainy to stay outside. The fire started to spit and sputter.

"I'll take the lean-to for now," I said.

"You're sure?" Laura asked.

"If it gets really bad, I'll squeeze into the tent."

"There's room," Jenny said grudgingly.

"Thanks," I said to her, "but I'm good for now." What I didn't say was that tents made me claustrophobic.

Laura disappeared into the tent, zippering the door behind her. I unrolled a sleeping mat and crawled under the canoe and the poncho.

I must have slept for a while, because I started awake at

something tugging sharply on the poncho, trying to get into my little nest. "It's me!" Laura whispered. I reached out and pulled her close, quickly arranged the poncho over both of us.

"Thought you might be cold," she said.

"A little," I said.

"You can hug me if you want."

We snuggled against each other and listened to the wind. We might have dozed—maybe for a long while—because suddenly a tree slammed *boo-foom!* to the ground not far away.

"My God, Jed!" Laura said.

"Laura?" came Jenny's plaintive voice. "Where are you?"

"Here!" Laura called.

"I'm scared."

Then another tree groaned and slammed to the ground; sticks and debris rained around us.

"Straight-line winds," I shouted. "We've got to get out of the trees, back down toward shore!"

"Okay! But I've got to get Jenny," Laura shouted.

"Hurry," I called. In the flashbulb washes of lightning I saw another pine snap off halfway up its huge trunk; in the foreground, the tent flapped and pulsed in the whipping wind like a heart, pumping faster and faster.

"Open the zipper! I can't find the zipper!" Laura shouted

to Jenny. *The wind sounded like a freight train.* That's what everybody always says, but it was true. This was no tornado but a freight-train wind roaring straight down the tracks.

I saw her struggling with the tent, then felt, or heard, a tree give way directly above us up the hill. Its roots groaned like an elephant in pain; then a ripping sound. In a brilliant flash, I saw the pine floating directly down on our campsite.

"Laura! Run," I screamed.

I lunged toward the tent, but pine boughs swatted me into the ground as if I were a gnat. A half second later came the concussion as the tree trunk hit the ground—which heaved up in a wave, like when the Iron Range miners blasted for ore, when an entire hillside shrugged its giant shoulder. I fought against things covering my face like I was drowning, like I was underwater. But it was pine boughs and prickly needles, a web of them, heavy, like ropes thrown over me, pinning me down, a fly struggling in a massive web.

I heard screaming. Screaming from where the tent used to be.

"Laura! Jenny!" I shouted. The lightning lit the sky enough for me to see the worst: The tree had slammed down alongside the tent, then rolled onto it.

I fought my way free of the webbing and scrambled over the massive tree trunk.

The tent was torn. I reached inside, caught a skinny arm, and pulled.

Groaning, whimpering, Jenny emerged. "Stay right here, alongside the tree!" I shouted to her. Around the campsite more trees slammed down like giant dominoes falling.

"Laura—she can't move!" Jenny screamed.

I tore at the tent fabric, felt the zipper rip my palms, and found a stronger arm.

"Oh God, get it off, get it off," Laura groaned.

"Where are you hurt?" I shouted above the raging wind.

"My legs, I can't feel my legs!"

I wrenched away the remains of the tent and felt for her below the massive, cold, wet trunk of the pine. Its bulk lay directly over her knees. I braced myself and tried to heave the pine; it was like one person pushing against a building. I scrambled around to the other side and felt her legs. Both were bent at wrong angles.

"We can dig!" I shouted to Jenny. I tore off a sharp branch. "Laura is stuck. Take this and dig. I'll do the same on the other side."

"Dig where?" Jenny cried.

"Underneath her. We've got to take the pressure off."

Using the strobe light of the lightning flashes, we scratched and dug at the earth like crazed animals.

"Ouch!" Laura cried once. "You're poking me."

Good sign. "Sorry," I shouted.

"I keep hitting rock!" Jenny said.

"That's okay, there's several inches of dirt. Get out all you can."

Laura was silent.

"Hey, you okay?" I called. I was making some progress.

"Whatever you're doing, it hurts more now," she groaned.

Even better. And then I hit bedrock. Canadian Shield.

I paused to catch my breath; my lungs were on fire, my fingertips too.

"So?" Laura said.

I looked over the trunk at Jenny. A mound of of dirt and pine needles lay behind her, as if a dog had gone crazy digging for a bone. *Laura's bones.*

"So?" I said. "You can feel everything?"

"Yes."

"Wiggle your toes?"

"I think."

I groped in the branches and mud, and found a bare, cold foot. "Do it."

They twitched nicely.

"It's all good!" I said.

"Well, not all good," Laura said, her teeth beginning to chatter.

"True," I said.

Jenny looked me, her face flashing white and very scared. "She's not stuck. She's pinned."

"Duh," Laura said.

"Could be worse," I called. My voice was suddenly very loud; the wind was dying fast, as if it had taken its best shot, its knockout punch, and now sagged limply against the ropes.

"I hate optimists sometimes," Laura said. She managed a brief laugh, then fell silent.

"Jenny, get that poncho. We have to keep her dry."

She obeyed, and I worked with my wooden spear at trenching around the Laura's body so the muddy rainwater drained off to the sides.

"Easy now," I said. We got most of one sleeping mat under Laura's upper body, then covered her with the sleeping bag and the poncho.

"That feels a lot better," Laura said with only a small groan.

"Now what?" Jenny whispered to me

I checked my watch; its green dial flashed 5:30 A.M. "I think we need to make a phone call," I said.

"In the Duluth pack," Laura mumbled.

"Take it easy, you're covered," I said.

"Yeah, by a frigging giant tree," she muttered.

Jenny smiled for the first time. Both of us rummaged for

the Duluth pack. "Here it is!" Jenny said. She felt in it for the cell phone.

Please please please don't be crushed.

Jenny touched a button; it beeped. "Here," she said; she handed the phone to me. Her eyes were wide and scared.

I took a moment to gather my wits. I didn't want to be on one of those 911 wilderness rescue shows, be the frantic voice on the "actual audio tape" they play over and over.

"Ely Police, Fire, and Rescue," said a woman's voice.

I was surprised at how fast she answered. She was breaking up slightly in the receding thunderstorm, but I could hear her well.

"Ah yes, hello," I said. Then couldn't think of what to say.

"What's the nature of your emergency?"

"Nature is the nature," I said. It was the first thing that came into my mind; I wasn't try to be a smart-ass. I got a grip and described what happened.

The dispatcher was suddenly all business. "Is she breathing?"

"Yes, all that stuff. She's stable and out of the weather mostly. But there's this giant tree." At that point, my voice broke.

"Are you injured? Tell me about you," the woman said. Her voice was warmer now, motherlike.

"No, I'm fine. Really. It's Laura—we've got to get this

tree off!" My voice rose again at the end. I forced myself to get a grip. In the background I could hear her speaking rapidly to other people. I gave her my location again.

"We're one hour from you by helicopter," she said lazily. "We'll need you to mark your location onshore with something, such as a fire, or something bright."

"A fire? How in the hell——" Then I got a grip. "How about a yellow kayak?" I replied. "It will be pointing uphill to the campground where we're stuck."

"That sounds just fine, perfect in fact. May I talk to Laura now?"

"She's a little busy right now," I said.

"Put her on if you would."

I shrugged and held the phone down for Laura.

"Yes, I can feel my legs. Actually, they hurt like hell!" Laura said.

When Laura began to repeat things I had already told the woman, I took back the phone. "She needs to rest right now."

"No, she needs to be kept awake," the woman said smoothly. "We don't want her to go into shock."

"I hear you," I said.

"That's what you need to do now. Keep her talking, chafe her hands, her legs, anything to keep her alert."

"Okay. I'll have her sister do that while I set out the kayak."

"Now you've got a plan," she said in the lazy, self-assured

voice. "And I can tell you that a rescue crew is boarding a helicopter in Duluth as we speak. Estimated time of departure, less than ten minutes. ETA, forty minutes to one hour, max."

"Cool," I said. "Gotta go." I handed the phone to Jenny.

Around us now the woods were strangely silent. Wrecked. Stunned. Thunder rumbled far off to the east. I made my way down the hill, following the trail as best I could, crawling over several giant tree trunks, and found the rock plate of the shoreline. The water had picked up gray light and I could see, like a bone, like a pale rib, the outline of the kayak. Even with its rope, it had smashed and battered itself against the landing.

I struggled to free it from branches and debris. It took a long time. I was in slow motion, running on empty, like I was trying to play tennis after not eating all day; my legs and arms were as heavy as green, wet wood. After I got it free, and upside down on the rock, pointed the right way, I sank back onto some tree limbs and caught my breath. I squinted closely at my hands; they stung as if bees were crawling on them.

Then I looked away. The skin and fingernails were torn from digging for Laura. I crawled to the water and submerged them. I groaned at the pain, but the icy water quickly numbed them. Afterward I sat back against a massive stone and, for just a second, let my head slump forward; for just a second, let my eyes close.

Chop-chop-chop. The helicopter's sound jerked me awake. I scrambled upright. Above the Kawishiwi was the chopper, and just below, on the gray water, came a powerboat.

"Here!" I called, which was stupid; none of them could hear me. But within a couple of minutes both yellow spotlights fell on me and the kayak with a brightness of the sun coming up.

The boat, manned by guys in helmets and backpacks, accelerated toward shore. I pointed uphill and scrambled there myself. I was suddenly ashamed at leaving Laura for so long.

"They're here," I called to Jenny.

"Cool," she answered.

She was sitting with Laura's head in her lap; Laura was on the phone.

"I told you, Mother, I'm fine," Laura said into the phone.

I was flooded with relief. Laura's color was fine, her voice was strong—we were home free.

"Up here!" I called over my shoulder. Chain saws snarled as the Forest Service guys fought their way uphill. Two EMTs, one a red-haired woman with a major pack of medical gear, hurried into the campsite.

"Hi, I'm Barb. What seems to be the trouble today?" she

asked as she knelt by Laura. She had that same lazy, it's-all-good voice as the 911 woman; I wondered if they had to practice that, if there was a class adults took called Reassuring Voices 101.

Laura managed a smile. "A tree got in my way."

"I guess it did, honey," she said, beginning to listen to Laura's heartbeat with a stethoscope as the other EMT strapped on a blood pressure cuff.

"Your helpers here can step off to the side while we work," Barb said, with a brief smile our way.

Jenny and I got the message.

Radios crackled. The second EMT spoke quickly into his shoulder-mounted transmitter; chain saws roared louder as men came up the rocky hill.

I took Jenny off to the side and sat her down with my arm around her. She began to tremble.

"You did a great job today, kid," I said.

She huddled against me and sobbed like a baby; I let her stay that way as we watched the rescue. Other men arrived carrying ropes, a stretcher, and all manner of logging gear.

"Stable?" a lean, bearded forest ranger asked.

Barb nodded. "Ready to go," she drawled, and stepped away. "Be careful with her."

"We do our job, you do yours," the ranger said. "Let's go with the hydraulic jacks—now!"

I couldn't watch. Couldn't not watch. The chain-saw guys first cut bright-yellow pine wedges to brace the tree from underneath. Two burly guys swung heavy sledgehammers as they pounded in the wooden blocks. Laura flinched with each slamming blow to the pine.

"You're fine, honey," the red-haired lady said to Laura.

Finally one of the rangers shouted, "She's not going anywhere now."

"Meaning the log, honey," said the EMT.

The loggers were sweating hard; the sun was brighter now, and below on the rocky plateau the helicopter's blades went *fwopp-fwopp-fwopp* in a slow, steady rhythm. It was waiting. Now men began to lop off the pine, starting at the top. Limbs and chunks dropped and thudded over the bank.

"Little bit at a time, that's it," the main ranger called.

The tree got shorter and shorter as the men neared Laura. Sawdust spewed yellow as the whining blades came closer to Laura's legs.

"Enough!" the ranger shouted.

The saw engines died.

"Now the big jack," he shouted. "Move the wedges in the second it starts to lift."

Jenny averted her eyes; I kept looking. That's because Laura's eyes were on mine; she was scared.

"Don't cut my damn legs off," she said.

"You're good, honey," Barb said. She was holding Laura's hand.

Then, miraculously, there was air above Laura's legs. The heavy dent in them, the flattened part, nearly made me sick. Both were broken, though still pink.

Laura tried to look, but Barb shielded her view. "Just keep looking this way. Everything is still there, if that's what you want to know. You're gonna be fine," she said.

Laura held on to her hand.

"Flat board," the other EMT called. "Go easy. Don't twist her."

Within a minute, Laura was extricated and strapped down like a mummy.

"Hey," I said, "you're going home."

She nodded and mouthed me a kiss. "Thanks for saving me," she said.

"It's what we do, right?" I tried to be cool, but my voice was choky.

"You too, Jenny. You did a great job."

Jenny began cry as they took her sister away.

"Coming through," the stretcher bearers called. The path downhill was clear and sawdust lined, and we fell in behind. I looked over my shoulder at the campsite. It was covered with fallen trees. The Wenonah canoe was crushed at the

stern, right where my head—and Laura's—had been. I tried
to recall our exact movements when the trees began to
snap: jumping up, leaping here, stumbling there. I wondered
what my dad would say about his canoe.

At the river's edge, we hung back as they loaded Laura
into the helicopter.

"Okay, now let's take a look at you two," Barb said.

"Just a sec," I said. "I want to see them lift off."

When the door was closed, the pilot gave a thumbs-up
signal. The engine whined harder, and the long blades picked
up speed until they whipped up a hurricane of sawdust and
pine needles. Blown against the rock face, the flying debris
engulfed the helicopter.

We shielded our faces, then, after the stinging rain of
debris ceased, looked again; the chopper had gained twenty
feet, then fifty feet, over the river. Its noise was deafening.

"She'll be in the hospital in no time," Barb shouted.

I nodded.

"Let me see those hands," she said.

I held them out to her—winced as she touched them—
which was the moment I took my eyes off the helicopter. It
was also the same moment that everything went quiet.

We looked up as one.

"Oh shit," someone said.

I jerked away my hands and found the chopper again with

my eyes. It was downriver now, flying in absolute silence. But not far away enough to be so silent. Its engine coughed once—twice—like a car trying to start.

"God, no," Barb whispered, "please no."

Then the helicopter tilted forward, in slow motion. As it tipped, the pilot tried to restart the engine again and again—all the way down—and was still trying even as it slammed nose first into the river.

A mushroom spray of water replaced the helicopter's torpedo shape—a simple matter of displacement, of physics, really. Water soared upward like a geyser, higher and higher, until the finest, leading droplets caught the sun. When the fist of water fell back, all that remained was the gray, flat, silent river.

CHAPTER TWENTY

It's not the big, tragic things in life that do you in—it's the small stuff, like not brushing your teeth. Not washing your hair. Not wearing clean underwear. Then, like droplets of oil on water, the small bad things begin to hook up and spread over everything.

Take my family the DedBeets. My virtual family, that is. They're from Echo, a computer game that Bobby Wheeler brought over. I play it continually. When I first started, I made my DedBeet family a house but forgot to add windows; slowly the family got depressed and didn't do well at work and school, the parents fell behind on payments, the husband started to drink, and now the two teenagers are in foster homes. All from having a house with no windows. I think one of my DedBeet kids is going start doing drugs or turning tricks, but Bobby said things like hard drugs and drive-by shootings are possible only if you buy the expansion pack StreetSmart. Anyway, my DedBeet family is in a downward spiral.

My real life is more like a circle. Because I play Echo all the time and don't take hygiene breaks, I have furry teeth, which makes my breath smell when I talk into the phone, so I don't return phone calls to people (such as my sisters and Mr. Stinson), who only want to know how I'm doing in general and how I'm doing at Oakleaf Alternative School in particular, neither of which I want to talk about because I'm playing Echo.

How am I doing really? Shitty would be the answer.

Or, to be correct, shittily. The adverbial form. I still have it, the school thing, but I couldn't give a damn, which did not make things easier when it came to the high school judicial conduct hearing, the juvenile court system, not to say Oakleaf Alternative School (you get the drift).

"This is crazy," I said to Vice-Principal Hartness at my hearing (rescheduled only two weeks after Laura's funeral). "Can't you see that?"

As it turned out, the vice-principal could not see it.

"One joint of marijuana that I found—didn't buy, didn't use—but found? This is totally insane," I said to the judge in my juvenile court appearance. "Can't you see that?"

Turns out he couldn't see it, either. I received a year's probation and came home "still angry," according to my counselor, Mr. Merkowski.

"Do *you* think you're angry?" said Merkowski, a man with

no capacity for facial expression.

"I don't know, do *you*?" I replied every time.

That old game. Now, during my weekly sessions with Merkowski, I never said a word. What was to say? I was still pissed off about our first session, the way he drew me out, got me to talk. One word led to another; first thing I knew, he had me spilling my guts about Laura. About how I blamed my father for her death. Shrinks love that shit.

Now I spend my time doing enough to get by at Oakleaf and playing with my little people, the DedBeets. The DedBeets are like a drug—I understand that, I'm not dumb—but so what? As the television commercials say, sometimes everybody needs a little help getting to sleep.

So far, it's six months after Laura died—gray November and the first snow imminent—and I still live with my mother. We remain in the big house, though it's for sale as part of the divorce proceedings. (I thought of giving a big house like ours to my DedBeets, but I'd have to find some cheat codes on the Internet because the DedBeets don't have enough money to buy a nice house, of course, because they're the DedBeets.)

I don't see my father. He has an apartment downtown. I wouldn't see him if he was dying of liver cancer.

I see Bobby Wheeler more than anybody. A couple of times a week he comes over and hangs in my room and I pick his brain about Echo and tell him the latest DedBeet news. All bad, of course. Sometimes when I call him, he says he can't come over, so I send him digital snapshots of my DedBeets. He has three Echo families going at once and offered to let me adopt one of his kids, Klever Kirby, a handsome, blond-haired, athletic boy who has good grades, many skills, plus an outgoing personality. *Like Laura, only male.* I considered adopting, but Bobby's thing is to continually improve his families—which is more or less the goal of Echo—so that they all end up with a mansion and a pool. A nice gesture, but I didn't think Klever Kirby would fit in with my sad DedBeets.

My two sisters began to come home and hang out with me on weekends, but it was clear my mother (and probably Merkowski) put them up to it. Melanie was sly about getting me out of my room to do things like wash my hair. They tag teamed me, pretending to be interested in the DedBeets, then saying non-sequitur things like how cool college life was, and how great it was to get away from Duluth and meet new people. But I was onto them.

And I was onto my mother. I understood, from bits and pieces, that the Sanborns were back together—how could they not be—after "the loss of their daughter" (funny how people can never say the word *death*). I even got an e-mail from Jenny, "just wondering how are you doing." I wondered who set her up for this—my mother and Mrs. Sanborn, I guessed, but I wouldn't rule out Merkowski. I knew for sure that the two mothers were in touch nowadays, trying to "salvage what they could," as my mother put it. The irony of those two communicating was beyond anything I had done to my DedBeets.

Eventually I sent a short reply to Jenny. It was the least I could do.

Hi, Kid,
I wouldn't recognize you without green hair.
J

Jed,
It was stupid anyway. I just wanted to be different. . . . I'm trying to picture how you look with long hair.
Jenny

(Long hair? How would she know that? I told you they all were in cahoots.) We exchanged a few more notes, but I wasn't encouraging. I told her I thought it was cool that she was doing well in seventh grade. We never talked about Laura or even used her name. And I was kind enough not to mention the obvious: Laura would still be alive but for her.

That point I saved for my father.

The heart of the matter, in other words.

What I couldn't get out of my head, what ran inside my

brain in an endless loop beginning when I woke up in the morning and still churning when I fell asleep, was this thought: If my father hadn't gotten involved with Mrs. Sanborn, *Laura would still be alive*.

Luckily Bobby got me started with Echo. "Hey, it'll take the edge off. Give you something to do," he said.

"What's Echo?" I said without interest. As a kid I'd done some Game Boy, a little Nintendo, but I was not a serious gamer.

"In Echo you create your own family. Pick names, pick body types, give them skin, personalities, hobbies—you name it."

"Sounds like something eleven-year-olds would love."

"That's Sims," Bobby said. "I used to play Sims all the time, but Echo is for adults. In Echo, nothing that happens in real life is left out. You can be totally cruel to them, force them into a life of crime, they can have sex, whatever."

"Little virtual people screwing—great," I said. "Why would I want that when I can go on-line and watch real people have sex?"

He ignored me as he set up the game. "I always wondered what went on in those houses in SimCity," he said. "I mean, building a city was fun, making streets, laying waterlines, but Echo lets you create people—like you're God."

Don't get me started on God. If there were a God, Laura would be a senior in high school, in class right this moment, sitting in the front row, laughing, raising her hand.

"Echo is the coolest game ever," Bobby said as he worked.

I stared at Bobby. He was really a very nerdy guy; it was a miracle we were still friends.

That night he showed me how to get started. I wanted to pick a ready-made family and house, move ahead quickly, get this over with.

"It's way more fun to make your own family, Jed. Any kind of family you want. "

And so losers from the get-go, the DedBeets, were born.

Bobby hung around late and explained the game, including the personality trait list, the mood indicator icons, how to buy stuff—it was best to start with basics such as a refrigerator and toilet.

"I only have a thousand dollars."

"So the dad has to get a job," Bobby said.

I made the father a septic tank inspector; gradually got the DedBeets out of an apartment and into a cheapo house (forgetting to add windows). First day in the new house, the mother went to the kitchen and began to cook dinner; things looked all good—until the oven blazed up red and fiery.

"What the—!"

"Whoa!" Bobby said, excited. "I've never seen that before."

"Now what do I do?"

"You put out the fire."

"How?"

"How do you usually put out a fire?"

I arrowed my cursor about the virtual house in search of a fire extinguisher. None.

"So you better call 911," Bobby said.

I scanned the DedBeets' house. "I don't have a freaking phone."

"That's because you didn't buy one and install it," Bobby said.

By the time I got the phone installed and the firefighters arrived, half the kitchen was charred and the DedBeets were in a total panic, jumping up and down and chirping in odd little voices that sounded almost real except that I couldn't make out the words.

"Cool," I said.

"I knew you'd like it. Totally strange stuff can happen— though if you think about it, most everything has a logical cause."

"So why the fire?"

"You never gave the mother any skills, cooking or otherwise."

"What if I had let the kitchen burn?"

"Your DedBeets probably would have died horribly, and

then you'd have to start over with a new family."

"Excellent," I said. One night with my DedBeets and I was hooked.

Except that it got old being cruel to them. I had purposely mismatched the husband and wife so they'd always fight; I made one of the kids neat and orderly, the other one a slob—but I made the slob very artistic, which annoyed the neat one. And so on. I also made the father's job get worse—from septic tank inspector to cleaning the tanks with a shovel—and I gave the wife a secret gambling addiction, so that no matter how hard or long the husband worked, they always had less and less money. Then the husband began to drink, the kids were taken away, etc.

I kept calling Bobby to tell him the latest bad news. He wasn't impressed. "It's way harder to improve your family," he said. "That's really the goal of the game—to improve life."

I remembered a moment, about six months ago, when life was perfect. And I hadn't even met Laura.

Just for the hell of it—I had nothing better to do—I tried to turn things around for the DedBeets. I started with a mirror. It just came to me. If I couldn't add windows to the house (there wasn't enough money), I could add a couple of cheap mirrors.

I was right. The DedBeet mother began to stop on occasion and look at herself; touch her hair; check her teeth. Sometimes she stood for several minutes and looked closely at herself in the teeny little mirror—it was slightly creepy—but slowly her self-esteem monitor improved, along with her hygiene. The mother began to cook more often; the father's mood rose slightly.

I turned my attention to the two kids, now in different foster homes, but it was tougher there to turn things around. Other kids picked on my DedBeet children, who wept a lot and missed more and more school. I considered various cheat codes on the Internet, the main ones being ways to score extra money, but by now I was no fool. Sudden "found money" would only get my DedBeet kids in trouble: Suspicions would be raised that my DedBeet kids were doing something criminal, or, if no wrongdoing could be proved, the cash would make the poor foster family jealous and angry. You get the drift.

One had to be careful about sudden moves of any kind.

Everything had to be earned.

Which was like a lightbulb going on.

And—can you believe it?—right in the middle of my epiphany, my mother rapped on my door.

"What?" I said angrily, not looking up from my monitor.

"There's someone here to see you."

"Bobby? Come in, man. I think I've got it figured out."

"It's not Bobby," she said softly.

I looked up. Turned in my chair toward the closed door.

There was some murmuring. "Jed?" a girl's voice said.

Please, no. Why do adults do this sort of thing?

"Jed?" she said. "It's me, Jenny. Jenny Sanborn." She didn't sound happy, either.

"Just a second," I called. I looked about my room. At the window and the drawn shade. Trapped. No escape. I pushed my sticky, lank hair behind my ears and opened the door a crack.

"I'm sorry," Jenny said in a rush. "They made me do it."

Behind her was my mother, white-faced and uncertain; below in the house I could feel the presence of Mrs. Sanborn.

"Hey, kid, come in," I said.

She did; I closed the door.

Her eyes traveled about my room. Her nose wrinkled, and then she looked embarassed.

"Sit down. If you can find a place."

She did.

I looked closely at her. "You've grown," I said. "You're, like, taller."

She smiled a little.

"And no green hair."

"That was dumb. Most of what I used to do was dumb."

"Happens to us all," I said. I nodded beyond the door. "Adults especially."

She smiled a little more.

"So they made you come all the way down here just to see me?"

"I e-mailed you, to warn you," she said quickly, "but you must not be reading your mail."

"Not often, no," I said.

"Anyway, I hate surprising you like this."

"Don't worry about it," I said.

We were silent for a while.

"So how's school?"

"Okay," she said.

I couldn't think of anything else to say. And then she began to cry. I went over and sat on the floor and put my arm around her. She leaned into me and snuffled and jerked like a shaken rag doll; I held her tight.

"This is so freaking stupid," she said, rubbing her fist across her eyes. "I think my coming here was supposed to help you or something."

"Beyond help, sorry, kid," I said. That brought a little blubbery, teary smile from her.

"Me too," she said.

"Well, there you have it," I said.

We actually laughed; it was as if we'd found the answer.

"But thanks for coming, kid," I said, helping her up. "It's good to see you."

"You too, Jed," she said. Her eyes traveled to my greasy hair.

"I'm okay, really," I said.

"All right," she said uncertainly.

"Hey, be good. Do your homework, that sort of thing," I said as she turned to go. She nodded. She paused in the doorway; she was beginning to cry again.

"What?" I said

"She——you and Laura. She told me all about you just before——"

I held up my hands defensively. "Don't. Please." I was ready to cover my ears.

She swallowed, then put her hand over her mouth and closed the door.

Me, I returned immediately to my DedBeets. I was on a roll before the interruption. I kept them moving——working, talking, doing all the right things——until dawn, but made little progress in turning their lives around. I slept a couple of hours, then dialed Bobby's number. I was poised to ask him how he did it——how his families were so successful. *If you think about it, most everything has a logical cause.* Yes, things had to be earned, but there must be shortcuts as well. Things I didn't know.

Bobby wasn't home. "He's in *school*," his mother said.

"Ah, sorry," I said. I hung up. What a hag. Then again, why

wouldn't Bobby be in school?

I kept pacing my room, feeling this strange buildup of energy, then decided to go for it—on my own.

I slipped down to the corner QuikMart—it felt strange being outside, especially in daylight—and bought a six-pack of Jolt. Enough caffeine there to keep me going until my DedBeets were at least partially turned around. Home in the kitchen, I fixed a bag of peanut butter sandwiches for my caloric monitor and headed back to work.

In my room, I cleared away piles of rumpled clothes and dusty CD's, I stripped down to my my shorts, I cracked all my knuckles, and I set to work.

By midnight, I had the mother working again—two jobs actually, and the father was less depressed because there was more money, so they could have a second car. The husband actually stepped into the kitchen and began to cook—I held my breath—but apparently his mechanical skills covered him for following a recipe: The kitchen did not catch fire.

By noon the next day (Saturday, I think), I had both DedBeet kids in the same foster home, which was a major breakthrough. I worked on their hygiene and self-esteem— even took a chance by having them sleep together. It was a huge risk, but I recalled Bobby saying that the really weird stuff like incest only happened if you bought some sort of bootleg, X-rated expansion pack. And the risk paid off. The

DeBeet kids' comfort level shot up a full fifty percentage points. The next night they slept not in the same bed, but in single beds pushed close together. It was touching—right out of a Charles Dickens novel. I felt something wet on my cheek, and realized I was crying.

You and Laura. She told me all about you.

I shook my head rapidly side to side and pushed away from the machine. I stretched, did a few jumping jacks, slammed another Jolt, wolfed a PBJ sandwich, and dug back in.

By midnight (going on my thirtieth straight hour), I was a DedBeet puppet master extraordinaire. There were no longer keystrokes, wires, sticks, buttons, or controls. There was no clear line where I stopped and my DedBeets began. My computer was a windowpane of clear glass, a doorway through which I had passed.

I was doing everything right by the family: hygiene, comfort, self-esteem, work skills. The father was lifting weights; the mother had bought all new underwear. For the first time the parents had sex. It was grand, consummate, complete (and totally under a blanket). I wept with pure pleasure. The whole family was gliding along like *a canoe on water, a green Wenonah with Laura behind* like a well-oiled machine *I kept wanting to look over my shoulder but what if she wasn't really there* being considerate of each other, doing all the right things.

Near dawn, I had enough money not only for a decent

house but a modest-size swimming pool in the backyard. The DedBeets had always wanted a pool—that was clear by the way the children immediately dove in and swam rapid laps up and down the bright-turquoise rectangle. The children's voices chattered along with the sound of water splashing. The parents slipped upstairs to make love.

I leaned back, overwhelmed. It was all good. The DedBeets were home free. I tipped back in my chair, breathed deeply, let my eyes close. . . .

Sometime later I heard tiny cries, like baby birds chirping. I thought of spring. *May in the BWCAW, the fine green mist of new buds on the aspens, "Nature's first green is gold / the hardest hue to hold," I should call Stinson one of these days*—my mind was like a runaway hard drive, spinning, processing everything faster and faster; until I woke up with a start.

On my monitor, ambulances were parked outside the DedBeets' house. EMTs clustered by the side of the pool beside the silent bodies of the children. The DedBeet parents clung to each other, swaying back and forth, and made weeping sounds.

I stared. My mouth made shallow wheezing sounds. I looked at my tidy DedBeet house, the perfect green lawn, the robin's-egg blue water of the pool. The children were dead.

Without looking away from the screen, I fumbled for the

phone and dialed Bobby. He answered; he sounded like he was speaking from underwater.

"My kids died."

"Whaa? Jed, is that you?"

"Who else would it be! My DedBeet children died! How is that possible?"

"Where'd they die?"

"In the swimming pool."

"Could they swim?"

"Of course they could swim. They'd taken lifeguard training for chrissakes." I could hear my voice rising, chirping, sounding like the DedBeets.

"Get a grip, Jed. There's something you missed."

"Not possible. I had everything totally covered."

There was silence. I heard him yawn. "Tell me about the pool."

"Pool is a pool, dammit. Diving board, patio furniture. It's not too large, the temperature is right."

"Pool ladder or steps?"

I looked. Looked again.

"What?" I said. But I'd heard him.

"I asked, did you put in some way for them to get out of the pool?"

I was silent. "No," I whispered.

"Then they drowned," Bobby said. He yawned again.

"I know they freaking drowned," I said, louder this time.

"Don't you see?" Bobby added. "They swam and swam until they got hungry and tired, and since they couldn't get out, they drowned."

I was silent.

"Tough luck, dude," Bobby said. "Now you got to start over."

I carefully hung up the phone. I stood up, looked around my room. It was a mess. Like a bomb had gone off. I had never lived like this. I looked back at the computer. On the screen there was a funeral going on already; the DedBeet kids were to buried in the backyard, which had now become a cemetery.

I walked over and powered down—didn't even quit, just hit the Off button. The monitor hissed and ticked, like the remains of a fire, and went dark. I stared a moment at the blank screen, then went to my bedroom window. It was dark. It was four thirty A.M. It had also snowed a little. The first snow.

At the door to my mother's bedroom, I paused, then looked in. The same pale orange light from the seahorse night-light. The same everything, except that she looked so small in the bed. And she slept far over, on my father's side.

"Mom?"

She woke up with a start. "Jeddy? What's wrong?"

"My children died."

She blinked with alarm.

"On my computer game," I added. "It's not a big deal."

She sat up fully. "Are you okay?"

"I want to drive downtown and see Dad," I said.

"Now?" She looked at the clock. "It's—"

"I know. But I just want to talk with him."

She swallowed. "You're okay to drive?"

"For sure," I said. I went and sat on the edge of the bed; I touched her hair, and she leaned into my hand. "I'm so sorry," I said.

My mother must have called ahead, because my father was up and waiting for me.

"Jeddy!" he said as he opened the door. His hair had gotten so white, I hardly recognized him. He'd lost weight, too. His cheeks were sort of sunken, which made the scar from my fishhook look whiter. Behind him the apartment was tiny; his drafting table took up almost the entire living room.

"Hey," I said.

"Come in," he said awkwardly. He made no move to hug me. I wouldn't have either, considering my hygiene level.

"So how are you doing?"

I looked out his window, which had a view of Lake Superior, all black.

"My little DedBeets died," I mumbled.

He was silent. "Your computer game, yes?"

I nodded.

"Your mother warned me. Told me, I mean," he said hastily.

"I had everything covered. I had it," I said. "I had it!"

Then I began to bawl like a baby.

"Easy now, easy," he said. He came up behind and held me. I sobbed like I did not think it was possible to do—as if I were throwing up, as if my insides were coming out.

"I know, I know, I know," he murmured. "I know how much you miss her. It came out—Jenny told us how close you and Laura had gotten."

"Close?" I said whirling, suddenly full of rage. "I . . . I loved her!"

There it was. Finally it was out of me. Finally everything was clear.

"And I think she loved you," my father said, holding me again, restraining me, holding me. "Jenny said so. She said you two were 'totally right for each other.' Those were her words, 'totally right.'"

Then I couldn't stand anymore. My legs wouldn't work. My father felt me sag and helped me through a small door to his bedroom. "It's a mess," he said.

"So am I," I answered.

He peeled off my stinky shirt and jeans, put me into bed. "Some sleep, that's the place to start. When you wake up, I'll make breakfast for us."

I was mute, dumb. I lay there in his bed. I didn't realize my eyes were closed, or even that I was sleeping, but some time later I woke up with my father alongside me. His clothes on, in bed, under the same covers as me, snoring softly. We were sleeping back to back and had moved toward the center to warm each other. At the window, around the edges of the shade, sunlight was leaking into the room.